Seismic Faultlines

Christopher Cox

Book Cover by Christopher Cox.

Paperback ISBN 978-1-7330186-7-8

Ebook available on Amazon.

Also by Christopher Cox

Hunt for the Fallen Star

A thousand years ago, a legendary starship with mythological abilities to traverse space disappeared....

Still reeling from his father's tragic death, Casey is persuaded by his brother, James, to join him and their best friend, Heather, as technical support for an archaeological dig in Central America. But after they discover an ancient starship and Casey inadvertently transports them across the galaxy, they find themselves lost in space and unable to return to Earth.

With everything alien to them, they must navigate a perilous star-scape fraught with space pirates, alien planets, galactic imperial forces, and foes with elemental powers. Amidst the chaos and political cover-ups, they discover the truth about the fabled starship—that its abilities of space travel are unequaled by any technology or spacecraft—and become targets of a galactic emperor's ambition to conquer the known civilizations.

With the galactic empire's sights set on Casey and the found spaceship, he must forge alliances if he's to save James and Heather, and escape. It'll take all their skills to evade the galactic military and prevent the onset of intergalactic war.

Non-Fiction Books by Christopher Cox

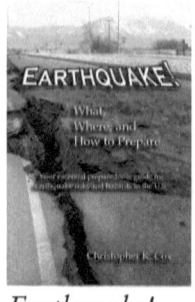

Earthquake! What, Where, and How to Prepare

Earthquake! What, Where, and How to Prepare was based on earthquake preparedness presentations Christopher gave. The book has three parts. The first covers the basics of earthquakes and their related hazards. Then, the risks and threats are reviewed for regions, states, and major cities in the United States. The last section goes into getting prepared.

Everyday Cybersecurity

Written for non-technical and "technology challenged" computer users, *Everyday Cybersecurity* simplifies computer and internet security. With the bad guys getting more cunning, it's vital that everyone who uses devices (computers, phones, etc.) to access the internet has a practical understanding and security awareness to protect personal information and identity.

To my dear wife, who continually supports and encourages my writing.

Thank you for reading *Seismic Faultlines*.

As an independently published author, you, as a reader, are vital in helping me as an author.

You're also key in helping others discover good books. Without a big publishing company and its marketing, independent authors rely more on you, our readers, to let others know you enjoyed our books.

When you're finished (or even before the end) if you liked my book, please recommend it to others and leave a short written review on the book's Amazon page.

Most people appreciate a good book recommendation from a trusted friend. Be that trusted friend.

And by leaving a review on Amazon, you can influence and help other people (beyond your friends and family) in finding outstanding books.

Once again, thank you!

Christopher Cox

Contents

"The Wasatch fault zone is the longest, most active, and most hazardous fault in the region. Movement on this fault has created valleys, like the Salt Lake and Utah Valleys, which contain the modern Wasatch Front urban corridor. The Wasatch fault zone borders and in some places crosses through this corridor, which is home to nearly 80 percent of Utah's population of 3 million and more than 75 percent of Utah's economy....There is a 43 percent probability that the Wasatch Front region will experience at least one M6.75 or greater earthquake in the next 50 years."

Earthquake Forecast for the Wasatch Front Region of the Intermountain West, https://pubs.usgs.gov/fs/2016/3019/fs20163019.pdf

Chapter One

Victory and Vengeance

C HANCE'S EYES DARTED ACROSS the field. Brett had just intercepted the ball. His stick twisted as he dodged an opponent's check and scanned the field for Chance.

Chance feinted left, and sprinted into an opening. Brett launched the ball downfield, heading off Chance in his dash toward the goal.

Ahead of him, four defenders raced towards Chance as he closed the distance on the crease. He reached high, leaped, and stretched his stick towards the blur streaking through the air.

He felt the mesh arrest the ball as it flew in. A defender stepped into him when he landed, and Chance spun around and continued toward the crease. He dodged a second defender and snapped the stick towards the goal.

The goalie dove towards the ball as it zipped past and into the goal.

The outdoor speakers blared the result, "Goal, Badgers! Fifteen to fourteen."

Over the bleachers on the sidelines, Chance saw the scoreboard change, breaking the tie, and noted the one-minute left of game time.

On his right, a defender caught the ball and instantly sent it flying towards a teammate on the offense. The offense caught the ball and rocketed it towards the goal. Ray, the Badgers' goalie, caught the ball and sent it to John near the centerline. John caught the ball in his stick's pocket, and wheeled around just as an opponent body-checked him.

The ball flipped out of the mesh, and another opponent snatched it out of the air. The offense catapulted the ball to a forward player, who sent it flying past Ray into the goal.

The announcer confirmed the tie. "Goal, Panthers! Fifteen-fifteen. Cory Evans has tied up the game once again with twenty-three seconds left."

Chance's jaw clenched. The Panthers were pouncing on his team.

Ray scooped the ball and yelled, "Chance it!"

The ball snapped through the air towards Chance near midfield. He easily caught the ball with his stick and started towards the goal. The field was open between him and the goal, but the defenders, who had spread out, were now closing in on him. His eyes zeroed in on the goal, identifying a potential opening on the goalie's left side nearly forty yards away. It would be risky, and a miss would mean they'd go into sudden-death overtime. Except for Ray, his teammates were struggling for the last several minutes, and another four would likely result in a loss.

His stick launched the ball towards the goal. The goalie reached out, just missing the speeding ball.

"Goal, Badgers! Sixteen to Fifteen"

The goalie scooped up the ball and sent it flying to midfield. Anticipating the intended target, Chance sprinted, jumped, and snatched the ball from its flight.

From the bleachers, loud voices counted down. "Five. Four. Three. Two. One!" Cheers erupted as the announcer proclaimed, "Game over. Final score: Badgers sixteen, Panthers fifteen. Congratulations Badgers!"

Chance stepped out of the locker room, turned into the hall, and nearly walked into Chad.

With his arms folded across his brawny chest, dusty hair cropped short like a sailor's, and a chiseled face, Chad looked like he stepped off of a youth magazine cover. "Nice game, Chance."

Chance nearly startled at hearing a compliment from Chad, then he saw the coolness in the eyes that wanted to bore icy holes into him. "Thanks. I didn't know you liked lacrosse."

"I don't. It's not a man's game. And from what I could see, I'm not the only one."

"What do you mean by that?"

"Well, if it were a real man's game, then I think your dad would be here. But since it's not football, it's not worth being here."

Chance felt heat rise in his face. "It was an off-season scrimmage, and my dad had to work."

Chad's mouth smirked, knowing he'd hit a pain point. "Yeah, about that. I don't remember him missing any of the football games. But how many of your lacrosse games has he come to? One? Maybe two?"

Three, thought Chance. Out loud, he didn't give Chad any satisfaction. "He's had to work more evening shifts."

The smirk grew. "Oh, that's the excuse he's given you. Well, if it makes you feel better, keep thinking that."

"What is it you want, Chad?"

Chad's cold eyes narrowed. "Not so much me as Coach Daniels. He said, we won't make it to state without you playing."

"Yeah, guess your team's losses prove you couldn't do it without me."

Chance could easily imagine smoke bursting from Chad's ears and blowing from his nose as muscular arms tightened around his chest.

Chad's voice was barely under control. "It's your fault, you self-righteous prig."

"Oh, it's my fault you and your minions were cheating in all your classes, and got suspended. And my fault you guys were hazing the freshmen."

"If you hadn't ratted on us, we'd already be qualified for the state championship. But you had the gall to be disloyal to your teammates."

The memory of the last few months was still raw. "I don't want to play football with you again. Not after all the lies and rumors you and your cronies started and perpetuated."

"Still," icy daggers glinted in Chad's eyes, "we can let go of the past, move on, and make our senior year one for the records."

"What do the rest of the team think about that?"

Casey could see a twist of resentment on Chad's face. "Most of the team wants you to play."

"As the captain, what do you think?"

Chad struggled to keep his words regulated. "Coach says you're probably the best wide receiver the school has ever had. He thinks you could probably get a scholarship if we have a winning season. If you play in college, he even said you could be better than your dad."

Chance noted that Chad skirted around answering. "But how would you feel about me playing?"

Veins bulged on Chad's arms. "I want to win state. Coach said I should easily get a scholarship to play college football, especially if we have a winning season. You," His head shook as his hands balled into fists. "You owe me. And you owe the team and school for what you did. If you want any semblance of a good senior year, you'll help us win."

Chance knew his answer, but simply said, "I'll think about it over the weekend."

Chad was about to reply when a nearby door opened and Coach Jarvis, the lacrosse coach, walked out.

Coach Jarvis looked suspiciously at Chad. "Is everything okay, Chance?"

"Yeah, Chad just came by to let me know something."

"Let me guess, Coach Daniels wants to make sure you'll be playing the rest of the season."

Chance started at the comment.

"Don't look surprised, Chance. Coaches talk. You have exceptional athletic ability. And Chad's an excellent quarterback. With the two of you on the same team, playing nicely together, you really could give the school a record-breaking season. You could still play lacrosse as well. You're still technically on the football team."

Suddenly, Chance wasn't so sure of his answer. "So, you think I should play?"

"That isn't my decision to make. It's yours. We could talk sometime. But right now I've got to be going. Have a great weekend, Chance! You really made some exceptional plays today. I'm looking forward to what happens when the season actually starts up. Chad, it's good to see you."

Coach Jarvis walked down the hall.

Chad's face looked smug. "Don't think too long about it, Chance. Remember my offer if you want the chance," he smiled at his witty comment, "of a great senior year. I can't guarantee it'll be very good otherwise."

Without another word, Chad turned and left Chance alone.

———

A few minutes later, Chance was approaching the exit of the school parking lot in his small sport utility vehicle. He slowed as several individuals began crossing the asphalt, stopped, and turned towards his vehicle. He recognized several of Chad's buddies standing in front of him. As he stopped, Chad walked over to his open window.

"Good evening, long time no talk," Chad smirked.

"I don't have an answer yet."

"Oh, I know. I just wanted to remind you of the generous offer. And add some incentives. I'm sure your dad would love seeing you playing a man's sport again. And your sister...what's her name? Oh yeah, Cassie. I'm sure she'll have a better sophomore year if you're on the team."

"She has nothing to do with this."

"Oh, contraire. Being in high school, she's directly affected by her older brother's actions."

Chance's jaw tightened. "Unless the world ends, I'll let you know on Monday."

"Better be early enough so that you can go to practice."

Chance nodded. Chad's head nodded, and he motioned his friends to the sides.

Slowly, Chance pulled up to the stop sign. His phone buzzed on the console. He picked it up and read the text from his sister: "R U still taking me to the mall?"

Chance's head dropped momentarily. With Chad's confrontation, he'd forgotten about getting home quickly to take Cassie to meet up with her friends at the mall. He quickly tapped out, "Had delay. On my way. Be home in about 30 min." Immediately, a thumbs up and happy face replied.

He set his phone on the passenger seat, turned on the radio, and turned onto the street to head home. On his right, the sun was sitting low on the horizon, just over the Oquirrh Mountains on the west side of the Salt Lake Valley. In the cool evening air, he debated about leaving the window down.

A song faded, and the DJ's voice came over. "Whoa, did you all feel that? For those who are near the Salt Lake area, we just had a little shaker a few minutes ago. Not the Big One, but the U of U reported it at a 5.2 magnitude. Hope you're all safe out there and nothing got too damaged."

Chapter Two

Fracture

Less than a minute later, Chance's phone buzzed again. After a near accident a year earlier, Chance almost never touched his phone while driving. He saw the brief notification that the text was from Cassie again. He wished his phone were connected to the SUV through Bluetooth, but he usually kept the phone's Bluetooth off because he was frequently targeted by bluejacking at school.

Ahead of him, the traffic light turned red. He slowed, stopped, and reached over for the phone. He pressed the power button and saw two notifications. The first was a low-battery warning. The second was the text notification. He touched the notification to read it and…HONK!

Behind his SUV, a vehicle blared its annoyance. His finger accidentally brushed the notification aside. He'd seen that it was from Cassie, but hadn't read it before the text notification was closed. Looking up, the light was still red. He glanced in the rearview mirror and groaned when he saw some of Chad's buddies in the vehicle laughing.

Another honk from behind and Chance felt his own annoyance building.

The traffic lights turned green, and the rude horn sounded again. He tossed the phone onto the passenger seat and figured he'd have to check the message at the next red light.

He drove on through the intersection. Through the mirrors, he saw Chad's teammates turn right. He felt his internal steam build when he realized they could've just turned right but intentionally pulled behind him instead.

Thoughts and feelings from constant harassment, bullying, rumors, gossip, and humiliation sickened and angered him. For over twenty minutes, scenes played over and over in his memory, like one of his grandparents' old scratched records on the turntable, while he continued home.

Chad's offer was tempting. Chance didn't doubt that if he accepted, Chad would not forgive him. He fully expected Chad to hold the grudge, but maybe his senior year might become tolerable.

The intersection light turned green as Chance approached. He turned left and began driving through the older section of town. The speed limit was slower than on alternate routes, but it was more direct, so it was fifty-fifty which route would be faster.

From the corner of his vision, he could see the slow blink of the blue LED notification light on his phone. He glanced at the dashboard clock. *Cassie, I'll be home in about 5 minutes*, he thought.

The steering wheel began vibrating in his grip, and he felt the SUV shaking. *Great!* His thoughts said sarcastically, *just what I need is car problems.*

The vehicles in front of him started bouncing and weaving. The old-style lampposts that lined the streets were shaking, and the few pedestrians on the sidewalks were in a panic. He even heard some screaming.

A harried voice interrupted the music on the radio. "We're sorry for breaking in, folks, but in case you're not in the Salt Lake Valley, we are experiencing an actual earthquake now." Chance could hear the voice tense up. "So far, it's been going on for nearly twenty seconds and has only been getting stronger. Everyone here in the studio is getting under cover as things are falling from shelves and dust is raining down from the ceiling panels. I advise all who are listening to find safe cover if you're indoors or a safe location outside, preferably away from any old buildings."

As the DJ spoke, the SUV rocked and bounced gently. Ahead and around him, the other cars were slowing down.

Chance realized the radio had been silent when a distressed voice spoke. "Is it stopping? The shaking seems to be lessening. Whoa, that was intense. I hope you all out there are okay. Here at the studio we've had a bit of a mess, but--"

As if on a dare, the earth undulated in spasms.

The SUV shook violently, and Chance fought to keep the vehicle driving straight as it flailed up, down, and sideways. Cracks split the asphalt as if a lightning bolt had struck the pavement, splintering the blacktop. Chance slammed on the brakes as the roadway in front of him broke apart and sank. His heart pounded with the trembling vehicle, its front tires teetering on the edge of the newly formed, massive pothole.

The outside discordance exploded through the open window, sounding like a long freight train speeding past. Piercing through the deep guttural groans of the earth came screams of terror and cries for help. Feeling like he had just been stunned, Chance's attention shifted to the surreal scene outside.

All the vehicles on the roadway had stopped. A nearby car was agitating in the growing pothole. The old brick facades of the historic buildings were spitting pieces of masonry onto the sidewalks. Branches and leaves shook vigorously on all the trees lining the road, and reminded Chance of deranged cheer pom-poms. The suspended traffic lights at the next intersection were trying to break free as they thrashed about on the cable. The unremitting earth convulsions stirred up and released dust and dirt into the air, giving the waning daylight an eerie orange-red haze.

An earthy smell, tainted with old asphalt and filth, snaked through the air and into Chance's nostrils. He coughed.

Deep grinding, punctuated with bass-sounding snaps, came from the left side of the street. Chance looked over and felt as much as he saw the thunderous avalanche of bricks crash down on the sidewalk and rush into the street, smashing into, and shoving vehicles away.

Through the exposed corner of the old building, he saw a parking lot full of vehicles twerking in a gravel parking lot. A nearby building, along with many of the larger buildings, was sinking into the ground that had an almost quicksand-like look to it.

An explosion happened somewhere in the neighborhood.

Down the street, on the right side, another brick wall collapsed and cascaded over the sidewalk and poured into the street.

Through the din, the breaking of windows stressed the dissonance. More screams.

Huddled in doorways, dread etched the faces of former pedestrians. A few people were in the street median, away from the buildings.

The ground turbulence escalated. Cracks spider-webbed throughout the blacktop. Concrete spat up from the breaking sidewalks.

Further down the street, several cars dropped from view. The walls of newer buildings showed signs of fatigue and stress. Windows continued to burst from their frames with the vacillating buildings.

Near where the cars had disappeared, a fountain of water spewed upwards, adding droplets into the granulated air, the moisture releasing a mold-tinged edge to the particulates.

The cacophony overtook the screams.

The pungent air, thick with earthen particles and mixed with remnants of civilization, assaulted Chance's nose and breathing. He coughed again. Inside the SUV, he felt like he was riding a wild bull and struggled to focus on anything but hanging on.

Explosive crashes started falling all around, sounding like a giant domino set tumbling. Chance's throat tightened when he realized he could barely see the buildings that had lined the road, and he was grateful he was in the street.

Suddenly, the front of the SUV dropped, and he felt the vehicle frame smash against the jagged edge of asphalt. The once-pothole had widened and deepened into a moderate sinkhole. *I need to get* out; he thought as he struggled to locate the seatbelt buckle amidst the lurching.

Beneath the SUV, the asphalt plummeted. Chance felt a moment of weightlessness before his head smashed into an enormous balloon that instantly appeared before him.

Chapter Three

Swallowed Whole

Blackness swallowed Chance. Something pressed against his face, and a strap pulled across his chest. Memory from before the black returned. He pushed back from the steering wheel and released his head from the airbag.

The air was thick and dark. Panic threatened to grip him. He wondered if he had lost consciousness and woken during the night. Away from the confines of the airbag, his eyes regained their focus. Shafts of light filtered down from above, through the dust-infested air.

His SUV angled down at the bottom of the sinkhole. The vehicle's front was smashed against a dirt wall, and the engine had stopped. His nose wrinkled at the smell of hot coolant mixed with steam. Looking up to the left, he could see the top edge was just above the back of his vehicle.

Other than the small hiss from the front of the SUV and some static on the radio, there was silence.

He pushed more and felt a twinge in his left elbow. Ignoring the pain, he kept his body weight back until he could release the seatbelt buckle. Twisting around in the seat, he pulled himself through the open window and climbed onto the SUV's roof.

Cautiously, he maneuvered to the back end and reached up to test the asphalt edge of the sinkhole. He broke off a couple of pieces until it felt secure and then pulled himself up.

Through the orange-red congested air, the remains of buildings appeared as apparitions in an alien wasteland. The trees had spectral forms that suggested unnatural origins. Shafts of setting red sunlight filtered through the brownish haze to create an orange-red.

Somewhere, crying children were hushed by the desperate and undecipherable words of a mother. Further away, someone howled. Groans came from the chaos of vehicles that cluttered the roads as survivors extricated themselves from their cars. A few looked at Chance. Some faces were almost expressionless. Others stood dazed, almost as if they were stunned by the unreal reality that surrounded them. He wondered if their bewildered expressions matched his own.

Near the rubble across the street, a young man clung to a young woman in an embrace. Dirty dust covered both of them. The sight of the young woman reminded Chance of Cassie.

He patted his pockets and then remembered his phone was in the SUV. Looking down at his vehicle in the darkening haze, he realized it wasn't in a sinkhole. The once-pothole had opened into a large fissure that split across the road and caused buildings on both ends to collapse. The jagged building ends in the thick air stood like precarious testaments to a fallen civilization.

He scrambled down, over the back of the SUV, and into the window. It took a few minutes of groping in the dusty dark before he located his phone under the dashboard. Then he crawled back and climbed out of the fissure.

When he was back on the remains of the roadway, he tapped his phone. The black screen didn't respond. He pressed the power button. The phone turned on and began searching for a signal. The logon screen appeared. As he quickly logged in, Chance noted there was five percent power and no cell or data service. He tapped the Messages app, and the phone powered off. A second attempt to power on the phone failed.

He wondered how Cassie was doing, and his father, who was working in Salt Lake City.

"Son, are you okay?" an age-encrusted voice asked.

Chance turned and saw an older man, who looked beat up, walking towards him. "Yeah, I'm good. My SUV's done for though."

"Probably wouldn't do you any good if it were still working," the man said. He pointed towards Chance's right forehead. "How's your head?"

"My head?" Chance reached up past his right temple and felt a dirty wet streak. He flinched a bit when his fingers encountered a tender spot. "It doesn't feel bad. I think I'm okay. Hey, is your phone working?"

The man shook his head. "There's no service. My guess is it'll be at least a few hours, maybe a few days, before there's some kind of service. Depends on how extensive the damage was."

"I didn't think the Big One would be like that."

"Son, what we just experienced would make the Big One cower in shame. I've no idea what it was, but it was way beyond the 7.2 Big One that scientists thought was the biggest we would get around here."

"Really? How do you know?"

The old man huffed a chuckle and coughed. "I've been around the world and was unlucky, or lucky, enough to be in Chile near the epicenter of an 8.5 earthquake. That magnitude was over ten times stronger than what our Big One was supposed to be. What I'm seeing here," his hands gestured around, "is far more devastation than what I witnessed there, and I'd bet the epicenter was on the east side of the valley, probably on the benches near the University of Utah. If I'm right, be thankful we're not there."

Chance felt his forehead tighten. "That's not too far from where my dad works near Salt Lake City." He turned to look northeast through the dirty haze.

The man's dark eyes examined Chance. "He was on shift this evening, wasn't he?" He coughed again and his voice softened. "A lot of buildings were seismically upgraded over the last several years. Hopefully, he's safe. But it'll probably be some time before you can call or text him."

"My phone needs to be charged first. I'm more concerned about my sister at home. Dad's ex-military and can take care of himself."

The man nodded. "Hopefully home's not too far away and she's okay. When you can charge your phone, remember to mostly keep it on airplane mode so it's not draining the battery looking for non-existent networks. I can't tell you how many times my phone drained quicker than usual when traveling because I forgot to do that. I've got to go check on some others and see how I can help. Good luck."

"Thanks."

Chance glanced at his dead phone as the man disappeared into the dust-choked air. After looking at the red orb of the sun that sat above the mountains in the west, he turned his attention to the street ahead of him. *Well,* he thought, *I've got less than an hour of light and a couple* of miles *to get home.*

Walking was easier said than done.

The first few minutes were spent trying to cross the fissure that split across the road. The collapsed remains of a building's wall ended up being the easiest passage across.

He passed several people. Most of those who were less injured were helping others. A man knelt on the sidewalk while he stared into the remains of a building. He heard whispers of a prayer as he walked by the still-standing entrance of another building, where a mother clung to two children next to her.

Vehicles littered the street, their occupants either still inside or standing nearby.

Pieces of walls and shattered glass spilled across the splintered sidewalks. Nearly every concrete walk section seemed higher or lower than the adjacent ones. Several times Chance scrambled over, or went around, piles of bricks and masonry that obstructed his passage.

A cool mist permeated the area near the broken water main. Water continued to spout into the air, and deep puddles had filled the many potholes that pocked the roadway. A light mud caked the surfaces. At the intersection, the back of a vacant car stuck out of a water-filled sinkhole.

On the opposite side of the street in the next block, a mid-size sedan had taken a small nosedive into a sinkhole. Cracks spider-webbed the windshield, while the darkly tinted back windows were still intact. Through the windshield, Chance saw two individuals slumped over in the front seat. He looked around and saw that he was the only one nearby.

Chance called out. "Do you need some help?"

There was no response from inside the car.

Chance sprinted to the car and assessed the situation. A young teenage girl stirred in the passenger seat. A woman, most likely the girl's mother, slumped over a deflated airbag on the steering wheel. Chance tapped on the tinted window, and the woman slowly lifted her head.

The ground began shaking again, and Chance's legs felt like jelly. Inside the car, the teenager screamed, and the woman startled, her eyes widening with fear. Chance braced himself against the car. On the other side of the car, he could see the sidewalk shudder and waves undulate through the masonry wall.

When the shaking stopped, Chance raised his hands and said, "I'm here to help. You need to get out of the car. That wall could fall."

The woman's head cocked and took a second to register what he said. Then she nodded slowly and unlocked the doors.

Chance lifted the handle and yanked hard to get the door to open past the broken asphalt. The woman started to get out but was stopped by the seatbelt. She looked confused about why she couldn't get out.

"Ma'am, you need to release the seatbelt," Chance said.

She blinked and nodded.

"Is she your daughter?"

Another nod.

"Okay, let me help you out. Then move beyond the building to that grassy section. That should be safe."

Chance helped the woman exit her vehicle. The teenager's door wouldn't open beyond the edge of the sinkhole, so Chance helped her over the driver's seat.

Chance walked with them past the building where they collapsed on the grassy strip. "The good news is it looks like you two are mostly just shaken up."

The woman's eyes widened. "My baby's in the back!" She stumbled in her attempt to stand as the shock of the situation shook her body.

Chance grabbed her arm. "I'll get your baby. You're not in condition to move very well."

Chance felt his own legs wobble as he staggered to the car. The nearly black tint on the back windows made it impossible to see inside. He opened the rear left door and saw a baby sleeping soundly in a car seat. He looked at the car seat for a moment, trying to figure out how it released, and heard several loud pops from the wall. Risking a glance, he saw waves undulate up through the masonry.

He found the car seat release and yanked the seat out of its cradle.

Louder pops and cracks emanated from the wall, and dust spat from the mortar.

With the uneven, shaking ground and trying to maintain balance with a car seat, Chance lumbered across the road towards the grass strip.

The wall fell down into a pile of rubble that pummeled the car. Windows shattered as old bricks broke through and bashed into the sides and roof of the car.

Chance moved the infant carrier in front of him, and he felt a rush of air and debris blow onto his back. Ahead of him, the child's mother screamed and then began sobbing when she saw the carrier. He set the carrier on the grass, and the mother quickly unbuckled the baby and lifted her into an embrace. The baby woke at that moment and let everyone know of her displeasure at seeing a stranger.

Chance smiled at the reunion, and the baby who had slept through a disaster. He looked back at the car. Bricks had beaten in the side and roof of the car, and some were even inside. His smile faded when he realized the mother had come close to possibly losing her two children.

Thoughts of Cassie returned to his mind, and he wondered what he would find at home.

Chapter Four

Ghost Town

THE SUN HAD LONG set when Chance finally made it to the street that would lead down to his neighborhood. What would normally have been a thirty-minute walk had extended over an hour as he trekked over the newly created rough terrain.

After leaving the older business district, he passed by other businesses and a handful of shopping centers. The lack of masonry did nothing to minimize the destruction. Signs had toppled. Walls and windows were cracked and broken. In a few areas, small groups of people had gathered to help each other. From a distance, he watched a smattering of individuals raid shops for food or electronics. He could understand the food as he guessed it would be days before any outside help came. As for the electronics, he just shook his head at the thieves' shortsightedness.

Normally, the streetlights would automatically come on as darkness set in. He had never really given it much thought before; the streets had just been lit. Without electricity, when the sun set, night swallowed civilization. By then, the heavy haze had settled to the ground, and the skies were clear, with only stars beginning to show. At one point he could see a lot of the Salt Lake Valley, or he could have if the electricity had been on. Instead of seeing the twinkling of tens of thousands of lights, there was a void. Only the silhouette of the Wasatch Mountains on the east side let him know the valley was still there.

The valley was not entirely an abyss. There were occasional specks of light, like lonely fireflies in the dark night. During his walk, he heard generators of various sizes running or powering on as building occupants attempted to re-grasp some kind of normal.

Abandoned cars littered the ruptured streets. He assumed their owners were walking, like him, to return home.

Chance's pace quickened as he walked down the main road to his riverside community. He grinned at the memory of when he used to think the Jordan River was a big river. And for Utah, it was moderate-sized. But after a road trip to the east coast several years ago, he realized that Utah's Jordan River was small, and some places in the country would call it a creek compared to their rivers.

Ahead, his neighborhood was pitch black. He slowed, not wanting to trip on the cracked concrete and uncertain about what he was seeing, or in this case, not seeing. In the distance—he couldn't guess how far in the dark—he could see a few faint lights. His pace slowed further. He knew several of his neighbors had solar panels and others had backup power generators. There should have been some lights in the void he was approaching, but there was nothing.

About a football field away, the ground disappeared, as if it were blacked out. With no lights, he approached cautiously. Then his heart sank.

The road and sidewalk ended in jagged tears. The entire area before him, as well as to the left and right, had dropped into a massive fissure. Stretched out below him under the starlit night, he could see the faint outlines of houses, or at least the piled remains. The roofs seemed to have fallen and collapsed in on their dwellings. Shredded and crumbled streets streaked the sunken neighborhood. Somewhere water splashed.

A knot tightened in his throat as he surveyed the dark devastation. Nearby, the building at the edge of the destruction had slumped and slid over, its roof creating a long, rough slide into the abyss. Not seeing a better option, Chance picked his way through the rubble to the steep roof-slide and slowly descended.

From the darkness on his right, he could hear the continuous splashing of water cascading from somewhere on the wall into pools below. A mix of smells bullied his nose with sewage, mold-filled earth, and hints of natural gas and gasoline.

His feet briefly splashed through liquid as he navigated the wasteland that was once his neighborhood. Twice he had to backtrack a block because familiar landmarks no longer existed.

Like most of the neighborhood, his house was a wrecked pile of construction debris. The roof appeared to have folded in on itself. Walls had buckled and were less than half their original height.

"Cassie!" he shouted as he approached. "CASSIE!"

He walked around the house pile several times as he continued to call for his sister.

Finally, he heard a reply, but it came from a few houses away. "Chance? Is that you?"

The voice was not Cassie's. In the night air it sounded heavier, thicker. "Mr. Stone?"

A shadow detached itself from the remains of a nearby house. "Chance, it's good to see you made it back home. Although, as you can see, there's not much left."

"Do you know if Cassie was home?"

The middle-aged man shook his head. His voice drooped. "I'm sorry. I have no idea. I was out back doing some yard work when the quake hit."

"Do you know who survived?"

Mr. Stone's voice lowered. "My wife was off shopping, and I haven't heard from her. You probably aren't aware of it, but most of the neighbors are gone on Friday nights, so I doubt there were very many people home. Was Cassie home?"

Chance could only nod.

Mr. Stone looked at the ground. "I'm so sorry. But maybe she found a safe place. As you can see, the houses aren't completely flattened, so it's possible. Would you like me to help you look?"

Chance shook his head. "I'll start, and if I need your help, I'll let you know. By any chance, is your phone working?"

"Not since the quake. I keep checking. And had to get it charged up a bit ago when it nearly died. I keep praying something will get back on so I can try to contact my wife." Mr. Stone looked up towards the walls of the fissure.

"You said you charged your phone. Do you have a battery pack I can use to charge my phone up a bit? Just enough to check a text from Cassie I missed."

"Sure. It's back at the house, well, at the rubble pile that used to be my house. I had to crawl in to get it. Good thing I have several around the house. Come with me. I got some things to eat as well. You're welcome to have a bit."

Chance followed his neighbor across the street and two house-remains down. Mr. Stone turned on a flashlight and swept it across the ground to find the battery pack and an assortment of granola bars, crackers, and other snack items that must have come from a pantry. There were also a couple of dirty blankets.

"Bet you're wondering why I didn't turn the light on earlier," Mr. Stone said as the light flicked off. He handed the battery charging pack to Chance as he continued. "I'm not sure who's around and don't want to call attention to myself in the dark."

Chance plugged his phone into the charger and within a few seconds the battery charging icon appeared momentarily on his screen.

"Do you think it's safe down here?" Chance asked. "I smelled some natural gas when I came down."

"It's probably safer than some places. Especially since it's harder to get to in the dark. How far did you walk?"

Chance related his experience and then asked, "So, do you have any idea what happened to our neighborhood?"

"No, not exactly. Although when I bought the land to build on many years ago, an old friend of mine cautioned me against it. He said he'd seen some survey maps from the mid-twentieth century that showed possible unstable ground along the Jordan River. It was his opinion that the ground under the riverbed and banks would likely experience some subsidence or strong liquefaction in the event of a big earthquake. I didn't listen to him and wanted to view of the river and park." He grinned. "And based on what you just told me, it probably wouldn't have made much of a difference if I'd bought land and built my house elsewhere."

After several minutes, Chance tapped the power button and was happy to see the battery was at ten percent. Holding the power button, he released it when the phone powered on. A few seconds later he logged in and tapped the Messages app. At the top was the unread message from Cassie. He breathed out a sigh of relief and then caught his breath.

"Is Cassie okay?"

"I hope so. She wasn't at home when the quake struck; that much I know. Her message said Jenna would take her." He made some quick calculations in his head. "Based on when the message was sent, about twenty minutes before the quake, she and Jenna were probably at the mall, probably with their other friends, when the earthquake struck."

"Any word from your dad?"

"No, he was working a shift in Salt Lake. I'm sure he's better able to take care of himself than most." Remembering some earlier advice, Chance switched his phone to airplane mode and then powered it off.

"So, what're you going to do?"

"Go find Cassie."

"You'd be better off waiting until morning to go."

"But she might be hurt and need my help. I need to get there sooner rather than later."

Chance could see Mr. Stone's arms motioning around in the night. "Look around us. And you know better than I that up there isn't any better. If you head off now, in the dark, over uncertain terrain, you're more likely to get yourself hurt. Then how will you help Cassie?"

Chance turned away, his hands balled into fists. His eyes squeezed shut for a moment, then opened as his head hung. "What if she needs help?"

"Most likely, there'll be people around who will help. But you'll travel easier and safer in the morning. And maybe you can scavenge something helpful before you head out."

Chapter Five

Smoke and Silence

THE NIGHT WAS COOL, and the ground uncomfortable. Throughout the night, his mind continually replayed the earthquake, and he worried about his sister. Several aftershocks woke him through the night.

One aftershock shook Chance violently awake. It rattled him for about a half-minute and subsided. Then the shaking intensified. For several confused seconds, he wondered if he was trembling from the memory of the previous day or shivering from the cold. In the darkness he heard the breaking of wood, broken houses settling into their debris piles, and rocks cascading from the newly formed ledges around the fallen neighborhood. Terrified cries rent the night air from a nearby neighborhood. The large tremor continued for several minutes. It didn't feel as powerful as the day before, and he wondered if the quake's epicenter was further away. Somewhere in his memory, he recalled his dad telling him the Wasatch Fault was about 240 miles long and actually had ten segments, with half of those being along the busy Wasatch Front where most of Utah's population lived and worked. He wondered if the aftershock had set off another segment of the fault.

He tried to return to sleep, but with his mind and body on edge, any remnants of sleep were gone. Over the eastern horizon a purple-gray fringed the mountains. He continued lying for a few minutes and watched the sky continue lightening before he got up.

Despite the lack of sleep, Chance felt more energized. He thanked his neighbor and spent several minutes attempting to scrounge through the rubble of his home. Most of the house's remains were too inaccessible without more resources and time. Under a corner of the collapsed garage, he found a couple of water bottles that had survived. Surrounding water puddles showed what happened to the rest of the case that had been near the garage door.

Chance temporarily powered on his phone to check the time and verified cell services were still out.

In the early morning sunlight, the long shadows amplified the destruction. He returned to where he had come down and cautiously scaled the slope of the roof back to the regular surface level. He turned and looked over the subdivision.

The rising sun was over the Wasatch Mountains, its rays piercing through wispy clouds as if everything should be normal. Below him, the sunken subdivision stretched towards what used to be a park and green space, and then to the river. The Jordan River seemed wilder, like an animal set free after being confined by civilization. Homes lay scattered across the area, piled like construction rubble. The once-smooth roadways lay buckled, torn, and crumbled. To the left and right, it looked like a giant plow had swept along the embankments to widen the river's path. During the night, the destruction had almost seemed unreal, like some horror that would vanish with the morning. He felt his insides churn at the realization that his home, his neighborhood, everything he had grown up with and known for the past several years, was gone.

His eyes scanned the east and north. Familiar landmarks in the distance, former buildings and tall structures, were gone or changed. Dozens of smoke columns billowed up throughout the valley, adding to the morning haze. Some were wisps, as if they belonged to campfires. Most were mixed gray-black plumes that likely came from building fires.

The quiet surprised him. He had grown up with the common sounds of vehicles and industrialized society. It seemed almost unnatural not to hear any cars. His head shook at that thought when he realized how backwards it was. As his ears attuned to the silence, they picked up a light breeze rustling some nearby trees and a few birds singing.

He took his bearings and felt grateful everything wasn't like his subdivision. The mall Cassie and her friends had gone to was about eight miles away. With traffic, it could be a fifteen-to twenty-minute drive. Based on his walk home, he figured he'd be lucky if he could get there in less than four hours. He looked at his water and took a sip. He would need to find some supplies if he were to get to Cassie and then...he realized he didn't know where they would go after that. Swallowing the water, he decided he just needed to find his sister and then decide what to do.

His mood brightened thinking of the bottles of water, protein bars, and a few other things in his SUV that could be helpful. The detour wouldn't add much time.

———

The return to the SUV was quicker than the night before. Chance figured the waning daylight and shock of the earthquake must've made him slower. The old business district was worse than he remembered and reminded him of a post-apocalyptic zone. He didn't see any other people. Cars were mangled by collapsed walls. The memory of rescuing the woman and her children sent shivers down his spine when he saw her car partially crushed under the bricks. The spouting water main had created a small pond and stream through the block.

He stood looking down at his SUV in the small chasm that split through the street and buildings. Water pooled at the bottom. His eyes followed the length of the fissure to the right, where the large crack started a couple of blocks away. He couldn't see the end on the left as it cut a jagged course through buildings and a residential area.

Chance climbed down and then into the SUV. He wormed his way over the seats to the back and sorted through the assortment of sporting gear. After emptying a pack, he put three water bottles and several snacks and protein bars inside. Looking at the various items, he added his team jacket and hat. He was about to leave when he remembered the two compartments on either side of the back. The first contained a jack and lug wrench, which he left. He took a first-aid kit and flares from the other compartment. After searching the rest of the vehicle, he added a flashlight from the glove box and his sunglasses.

On his way again, Chance figured he still had close to three hours before he got to the mall. He considered the primary route, which would take him east along Bangerter Highway and then north on Interstate 15. Driving it could be five minutes faster than the alternative, but it was longer, especially after his detour. He continued north on Redwood Road towards the interchange. Like every other road he had walked, vehicles of all makes and models littered the cracked and crumbled surface. Most were vacant, but a few curious eyes watched him as he trekked by.

Redwood Road vanished under the fallen Bangerter overpass. He approached cautiously. Cars were flattened under the weight of the demolished interchange. With roofs smashed in, it was unlikely anyone survived. He walked around the east side and crossed over. The collapsed overpass had swallowed several vehicles from Bangerter. A large cargo truck had crashed into a smaller coupe. His dry throat swallowed when he saw the profiles of drivers slumped over in their vehicles. A pang of guilt swept through him as he slowed down and wondered if he should stop and see if there was anyone he could help. His head drooped as he picked up his pace again and headed north.

A few blocks later, he walked through a fissured intersection. A tattered gas station sat on one corner. Behind the gas station, an extensive shopping center with a big box retail store stretched out behind the station on his right. A whiff of gasoline lit through his nose, which crinkled at the fumes. Two small crowds had gathered in the retail parking lot. Several people were gesticulating wildly with their arms and pointing at others who had full shopping carts. A half-dozen people were exiting the store while more were entering.

Bang! Bang! Bang!

His head dropped at the sound of the gunshots. Screams and discord instantly followed. A glance towards the parking lot revealed that most of the crowd were running, but a few had taken cover behind vehicles. He could see several handguns and assault rifles among those who remained. A body lay sprawled on the ground near one of the full shopping carts.

Several more shots fired, and Chance sprinted away to distance himself from the scene.

He briefly wondered if he should go through the residential neighbors and avoid the businesses, but decided continuing north on Redwood Road would likely be better than navigating unfamiliar streets.

Where are the cops? He thought, his mind dazed with what he had seen. A block away, his pace slowed to a walk. Dark smoke billowed behind a tree-lined neighborhood on the left. *And the firefighters?*

The unpleasant answer popped into his mind; if the roads were impassable, it was unlikely there would be law enforcement or rescue for at least several days. He would need to be on guard, especially as he got closer to commercial districts.

Chapter Six

Shadows in the Rubble

T HE REMNANTS OF SEVERAL restaurants caused Chance's stomach to grumble its displeasure at his inattention. Unlike in the previous parking lot, he didn't see any crowds. He reasoned that if he could find some food, then he could save his few supplies and it wouldn't be much of a detour.

He crossed Redwood and zigzagged through the cars of the parking lot towards a Mexican restaurant. After approaching the building, he immediately turned away when the odor of spoiled food assaulted him. He wasn't that desperate.

The next restaurant's food storage doors were jammed shut. Exiting the damaged building, he noticed a grocery store in a small shopping plaza across the street.

He watched the parking lot for a moment. When he didn't see anyone, he crossed over and headed towards the store, walking around the assortment of parked vehicles. Something felt wrong. *Maybe they're out of food*, he thought.

Near the store's main entrance, something long and slender curved into a large circle ahead of him. A few steps later he froze when the head of a large python lifted to watch him, its tongue flicking out. Chance backed off and gave the snake plenty of distance. He figured it probably wouldn't hurt him, but he didn't want to take any chances. The building next to the grocery store, its windows and doors shattered, had the broken sign of an exotic pet shop.

Stepping through the broken glass doors of the grocery store, he stopped mid-stride. Several bodies lay on the floor amidst the broken glass, fallen ceiling tiles, and collapsed display shelves. Some looked like they could have been victims of the falling debris, but others did not.

It took a moment for his eyes to adjust to the dimmer light. Without electricity, the only light in the store came through the broken storefront. In the shadowy store, he could barely see that most of the display shelves had shed their contents across the floor. Puddles of unknown liquid pooled among the clutter of packaged foods.

A couple of flashlight beams flashed and swept around the back of the store. Chance dropped low and watched the beams illuminate the backs of the mangled grocery aisles. Behind the closest cashier stand, a bakery display had spilled its contents across the floor. It wasn't far, and he figured he could easily grab a bag or two and be out before anyone saw him.

Ducking behind some checkout counters, he moved in towards the fallen display. The light beams stretched and shrunk across the back wall while he inched towards the nearest bags of rolls. His eyes were becoming more adjusted to the dimly lit store, and he noticed bottled drinks strewn across the aisle behind the display. The shelves on both sides had bent into the aisle and shed most of their contents. *A sports drink would be nice,* he thought, and he moved towards some bottles on the floor at the end-cap display. Smiling, he picked up a grape sports drink, unzipped his pack, and stuffed the bottle in. He grabbed a second bottle and then put the rolls in on top.

"I can't open the safe. How about the pharmacy?"

The gruff voice that called out was moving along the adjacent aisle. Chance froze at the end of the aisle.

Another voice, tinged with a thick accent, replied from the right side of the store. "It's locked as well. But I think your gun could bust the lock."

Chance felt like his heart was in his throat. Not seeing either person speaking, he dropped and scooted back into the aisle.

"Hey," said the first voice, much louder than before. "Where's Pete?"

A third voice responded from the store's left side. "I'm over here taking a whiz."

"You're supposed to be on guard until the rest get here."

"Relax. I was gone only a minute. If anyone got in, I can take care of it."

"Tom, are you going to help me with the pharmacy?" the second voice said.

"Chuck," the first voice called out, "leave the safe for now and get up here to watch with Pete. I'm going to see if we can get something worthwhile from the pharmacy."

A fourth voice, Chuck, responded from the back of the store. "Why don't we just hit the bank? There's more money there."

Chance could almost hear Tom's voice shake with annoyance when he responded. "There ain't no way we're getting into that safe. Most likely, the entire building could collapse, but the safe would be intact. We're better off here."

"You sure the cops ain't coming?" Chuck asked, his voice getting closer to the front of the store.

"Yeah. Not today. Probably not for a few days. They'll be dealing with saving the weak and checking their own families. And even if they weren't, the roads are undrivable." After a moment's pause, Tom continued, "Ahh, good. The others are here."

Sweat trickled down Chance's temples. He looked through the broken storefront windows into the parking lot and saw several men walking towards the store. Each carried a firearm. He would need to find another way out. In a crouch, he started moving to the back of the store.

Bang! Bang!

It felt like an electric shock struck through his spine when the two shots rang out through the store. He was near the back end of the aisle, and his eyes shot to the front. A couple of silhouettes were backlit from the storefront as they paced. He then scanned the back wall. Satisfied that nobody was at the back of the store, he located the employee door and passed through into the back room.

A few streams of light pricked through breaks in the exterior walls and ceiling. The meager light was enough to see an office door busted open. With his eyes more accustomed to the dimness, he could make out a safe in the far wall. *Better find the exit before those guys decide to come back*, he thought.

Boxes and cases were tossed about the back room. But despite the mess, the exit was easy to locate. Behind some toppled cases, the battery-powered emergency exit sign emitted a sickly green into the poorly lit area. Breathing a sigh of relief, he dodged the debris and scrambled to the door. Pushing the release bar did nothing. He tried again and couldn't budge the door.

After a third failed attempt to open the door, he stepped back to examine the door for a lock. The bolt was locked, but opening it failed to release the door.

Panic gripped his throat, and his heart pounded harder. He stepped back again and noticed the metal door jamb was bent in several spots. There was also a pinprick of light in the center of the door at eye level. Peeking through the peephole revealed the back loading dock. Like the inside, the dock was a mess. Several large objects pressed against the door.

He stopped himself from swearing when he realized that even if the door wasn't jammed shut, it probably wouldn't open.

"Let's try the safe one more time." Tom said as a beam of light swept across the back room.

Chance dropped into a crouch and turned in the direction he had come from, where he saw several shadows moving near the office. His eyes darted across the back room until they spotted the other employee door into the main store area. Keeping the piles of boxes between him and the office, he ducked around the debris field to the swinging doors.

Cautiously, he pushed one side. The door mildly resisted as it opened into the store. The opening was nearly wide enough to allow him through when it squeaked a loud complaint.

Chance froze.

Light beams flashed across the back room, and he heard Tom ask. "What was that?"

"Probably nothing," replied a voice Chance hadn't heard before.

"Take Mo and make sure," Tom said.

In front of Chance, he held the door open just enough for his body. He shifted his body and hurried through the door while holding it open. Light beams were scouring the back room and getting closer. In front of him, a short hall led from the employee doors into the main store. He could see light from the storefront and the back-lit shadows of shelves and scattered inventory that littered the floor.

The door yelped loudly when he let it go, and it repeated the cry when it swung back. Chance sprinted into the back aisle of the store and turned left to head to the front along a parallel aisle.

The door creaked again.

"That one was just us, Tom," said a rough voice. Chance guessed it was probably Mo. "Someone must be in the store. We'll check it out."

Chance felt the thump, thump of his heart pounding in his ears.

"Chuck!" Mo's voice shouted, "Pete, and the rest of you guys, scout the store. Someone's in here. Whoever it is, shoot 'em."

Shadows moved across the storefront floor. Chance looked forward and back and crept forward. He stooped and retrieved a couple of canned foods from the floor while he continued to the front. As he neared the front end of the aisle, a shadow moved around the bent end-cap into view. Without hesitation, Chance launched one can.

The can landed with a smack on the man's face. His head jerked back. The handgun dropped from his grip as he stumbled back and fell to the floor.

"Pete's down!"

Adrenaline shot through Chance. He scooped up the handgun as he darted past the end-cap.

"There he is!"

Chance ducked behind the last checkout stand as several rounds shot at him. Peeking over the check stand resulted in more rounds fired at him. He had seen three men moving towards his position. From the end of the check stand he fired several rounds at the men, and they retreated to cover. The check stand above him tore apart when a dozen rounds ripped into it. Glancing down the aisle, he saw two individuals moving towards him. He fired the handgun twice, and the lead man stumbled forward, grasping his left thigh. Chance pushed back to get better cover. He looked out at the parking lot.

Shreds of the checkout stand showered around him as more rounds fired into his cover.

Keeping his head low, Chance sprinted towards the broken store doors. Firearm rounds continued to chase after him. He dodged around parked cars while he raced to the end of the shopping plaza. Vehicle windows shattered around him. He skidded to a halt and jumped back when a muscular man holding an assault rifle stepped around a van to confront him. Holding the second can, Chance weaved around several cars. The man chased after him. Chance ducked behind a large truck and dropped low to watch the man's feet approach. Chance slowly moved around to the other side of the truck, aimed, and rocketed the can at the man.

The can thumped into the back of the man's head. He lurched forward. The assault rifle dropped from his hands, and he tottered towards, and tripped over the coiled python. Unhappy with the man's intrusion into its sunning, the snake expressed its displeasure.

Chance didn't stay any longer. Several of the other armed men exited the store and fired in his direction. He took off on an eastward run, thankful he was comfortable running distances.

It was several minutes before Chance slowed down. He kept more to the sides of the road as the grassy areas seemed less obstructed than the broken road. Ahead of him, the road curved northeast and dropped to a bridge that crossed the Jordan River. He was glad to see the bridge intact and that the riverbed had not sunk like his neighborhood. He slowed briefly to remove his pack while he walked. With the handgun still in his right hand, he slowed his walk enough to remove his pack. While his breathing and pulse rates returned to normal, he briefly examined the gun—a 9mm Smith and Wesson—and was thankful his dad had taken him shooting plenty of times. After setting the gun in the pack, he swung it back on and resumed his walking pace.

He was less than a block away when he heard a rumble, like continuous rolling thunder, from the south. He looked upriver and saw a roiling wall of water, a massive wavefront that raced downstream. Trees, houses, and even cars churned into the dirty tsunami-like wave that eagerly tore through the riverbed.

Chance looked across the bridge and back at the floodwaters.

Chapter Seven

Bridge to Nowhere

CHANCE RACED TOWARDS THE bridge in a desperate sprint. Somewhere in his mind he recalled floodwaters averaging six to twelve miles per hour. With the raging water about a mile away, he figured he had five minutes to get across the bridge to safety. Ahead of him, the road descended to the bridge, and beyond that it gradually rose back up.

The rush of water roared as it raced Chance to the bridge. A glance told him the monster flash flood was closer and much faster than twelve miles per hour. The bridge was still a football field away, and then he'd need to cross and get at least a half mile beyond to be out of the flood zone.

He skidded to a halt, reversed direction, and bolted back up the rise.

A breeze from upstream brought with it the odor of the turbulent waters that mixed with the land-based flotsam. The thunderous pounding, like the torrential sound at the bottom of a massive waterfall, increased.

I'm not going to make it, Chance thought when he stole another glance. *It's way faster than I thought.*

His legs burned with the continuous adrenaline, and his lungs felt like they were on fire. In his left peripheral vision, the flood wave loomed, jumbling trees and vehicles in the thrashing mess. The wind carried a foreboding mist that further saturated his sweat-soaked clothes. Behind him, vicious water thrashed violently, and for a brief instant he heard the deep crack of the bridge snapping apart. The slow floodwater edges slammed into his legs as deep energy reserves surged a last burst of speed into them.

Thrown sideways into the water, he rolled in the churning mess a short distance to where the riverbed turned northeast briefly before returning to its northward flow. The roiling waters rushed over the small ridge and tossed Chance into the remains of the residential neighborhood that had once lined the top.

He rolled over and fought his way to stand in the knee-deep water that whirled around the buildings. After moving further uphill, he turned and surveyed the river.

The once-small Jordan River now raged wild and stretched nearly a mile across from where he stood. From what he could see, the flood would continue, and he wondered where all the water had come from. There had been no rain, especially not enough to warrant the amount of water he saw. It seemed as if the upstream reservoirs had sent all their water downstream. In both directions, the dirty water looked more like a storm-tossed sea.

For a moment he wondered if Mr. Stone had escaped. Then, his thoughts returned to his sister. *Where to cross now*, he thought.

Upstream, the river had swollen to fully engulf the entire width of the river's course. The once expansive park and golf course that bordered the river were completely inundated. On the downstream side, to the north, the small river valley was not as wide. Where it could, the river expanded to fill in the lowest areas, flooding residential and business buildings.

Neither direction looked promising. Somehow he needed to cross the river, or wait for the flooding to subside. His thoughts returned to the bizarre idea of reservoir dams breaking. The Jordan River flowed from Utah Lake. Most of the water that entered Utah Lake came from the Provo River, which ran through two reservoirs. *What if*—his thoughts shuddered—one or both *dams failed? It'd probably take days or maybe weeks for the water levels to drop.*

Cassie was north and east of his location. He guessed another hour and a half would have gotten him to the mall, if he'd been able to make it across the bridge. Finding a river crossing to the south seemed less likely, and it would take him further from Cassie. He continued north to see where he could cross.

———

An hour later he stood looking over the newly widened Jordan River. Beyond Interstate 15, on the other side of the river, he could see the mall. He spent the next quarter-hour trying to determine where he could cross. He considered finding some kind of boat but quickly dismissed the idea when he saw uprooted trees and rooftops rushing by in the fast-flowing current. Even if he survived, he would probably be a few miles downstream before he reached the other side.

He sat down to rest and think, and removed his pack. The dryness in his throat reminded him he had drunk nothing recently. After unzipping the pack, he rummaged through it and stopped at the two bags of rolls, or what were rolls. Water had seeped into the store bags. He removed the soggy roll bags and was about to toss them aside when guilt struck. First, he realized he'd essentially stolen the food from the store, but he rationalized that if he hadn't taken the rolls, they would've been stolen by somebody else or gone to waste. And then, even with everything wasted around him, he couldn't bring himself to just litter.

Behind him was a series of quake-ravaged commercial buildings. As he walked to the buildings, he dumped the bread on the ground, figuring he'd at least feed some animals. Near the closest building, a dumpster had rolled away and got caught in the fractured parking lot. He opened the lid and tossed the bags in. After closing the lid, his nose caught a whiff of something that wasn't from the dumpster. It was the smell of something cooking.

Cautiously, he moved to the front corner of the building. Across the street was a large parking lot surrounded by a dozen stores and several restaurants. He hesitated when he saw a small crowd gathered between two of the restaurants. A thin wisp of smoke trickled upward from within the crowd. He was surprised when the crowd burst into laughter and applauded. Curious, he walked towards the gathering.

When Chance arrived a couple of minutes later, the crowd had broken into small groups. A peaceful line had queued up to two fires. Several people were cooking over the makeshift fire pits, and others were distributing food.

Chance walked to the back of the line and asked a gray-haired man what was going on.

The man turned and smiled. "We're getting a little something to eat. The restaurant owners decided it'd be best to cook everything up and have it eaten rather than let it go to waste. There were some looters earlier, but after the neighborhood got together, they left for easier targets."

By the time Chance got to the front, a couple dozen new arrivals were behind him. Six people tended the fires and cooked. Another half dozen were distributing the food. He could see that a variety of food was being cooked. Over some coals, hamburger meat was being browned. Fish and chicken roasted nearby. The line split into six, and Chance went to the next person.

A woman wearing a dirty apron smiled at Chance. "Sorry about the less than ideal cooking conditions, but if you don't mind it, you're welcome to a bite to eat. We're all in this together, so we just ask that you be mindful of others."

"Smells good," Chance said. "This is a great service you're providing."

Tiredness flashed behind the smile. "It's the least we can do. And probably all we can do since it'll probably be days before we get any outside help. From what you see," she waved at a table where a couple dozen disposable plates sat, each with different food items, "what would you like?"

"I'd appreciate the taco plate."

The woman retrieved a plate with two small tacos and a slice of apple. "There you go."

"Thank you."

"You're welcome, and God bless you."

Chance graciously took the plate and moved towards the perimeter of the gathering. After what he'd seen and experienced earlier, the peaceful gathering amazed him. He took a few bites and watched. To the north was an east-west six-lane highway. He had come from the east side, across a small street that began at the highway and went south.

Along the north, west, and south fringes of the parking lot were several groups of men holding an assortment of firearms. He nearly choked as panic briefly gripped him. Then he realized the men were guarding the area. Whenever someone or a group of people approached, the men would stop and talk to them. Most times, the stopped individuals were allowed through. In several instances, those wanting in handed over a gun or two before they could pass. He saw only one person who seemed aggravated and stormed away. When that happened, the guard who had confronted the individual used a radio to communicate something.

When he finished eating, he brought the plate back to the fire to be burned. "Thank you," he said to the man who took his plate.

"Glad we could lift your day a bit."

"Hey, do you know how I might cross the river now? My sister's on the other side, and I'm trying to figure out how to cross with the flooding."

"I don't know. But one of the guys on the north side—I think his name is Jason—might know. He's got radio connections around the valley and is probably the best source of information."

"Thanks again."

Chance made his way to the north end of the parking lot, to where a couple of ATVs were parked, and approached a group of six men who were watching the highway. "Is one of you Jason? I was told he might help me out."

A middle-aged man wearing canvas camouflage cargo pants and a light green shirt stepped towards Chance. The man had a radio clipped to his belt alongside a holstered handgun. An AR-15 that reminded Chance of his dad's was slung over his shoulder.

"I'm Jason. What can I help you with?"

"I'm Chance. I need to get to the other side of the river. My sister Cassie's over there, but with this flooding I'm not sure what the best way is."

"I'm not sure about that either. Definitely not here. We got the flood warning early this morning. Apparently, the big tremor we had near daylight this morning was a monster quake in Utah County, similar to what we had yesterday. I've got a buddy near Heber City who warned me the Jordanelle Reservoir abutments were compromised. And with the two quakes and the onslaught of water, Deer Creek's dam also failed. It'll probably be a few days before the water from the reservoirs has sufficiently drained."

"That's not good."

"You think we have it bad? I got some reports from Utah County, specifically Grandview Hill in Provo. They still had some power yesterday after our quake. This morning's took out their power. And he said the Provo River washed out of Provo Canyon at heights of over one hundred feet, and then the river flooded all the lower sections of the city, especially on the east side because I-15 created a partial barrier. But once the water started funneling through the east-west underpasses, Provo's west side got flooded."

"But what about crossing here?"

"Not an option if you want a chance to live." He thought for a moment. "But you might have a better chance further north, though you won't avoid the water. There's a spot where the river valley narrows before it widens. That's where I'd try."

"Guess I'll try my chances going north."

"Good luck."

"Thanks. Oh, one last thing. Do you know how conditions are near downtown Salt Lake? My dad, Doug Morgan, was working yesterday in that area."

Jason's expression turned grim. "It's bad and getting worse. My buddies in the area said to avoid the downtown and nearby areas at all costs. It's a disaster zone with severe damage and destruction in most areas. All the buildings are damaged, and many have fallen. Roads are broken and split apart. Large cracks divide the city. Utilities and infrastructure are completely severed. There are several out-of-control fires. And with each big aftershock, things get worse. There's no official count, but it's estimated thousands have died and many times that number are severely injured. Unfortunately, without the ability to get aid in there, it's likely many of the injured will die. As long as the fall weather stays nice, there's a chance. But with winter around the corner, things will probably get real bad, real fast. Compared to here, where we have to be on guard, in many places in and around Salt Lake the gangs are taking control. I'm sorry, but if your dad was in that area, it doesn't look good."

Chance felt like he'd been punched in the gut and a massive weight thrown on him. He nodded. "Thanks. Good luck to you, too."

About a mile and a half later, after skirting along the flood banks and debris for nearly an hour, Chance saw a possibility.

Chapter Eight

Warnings

THE RIVER'S SHALLOW VALLEY widened considerably at this point in its course. Although submerged, Chance knew there was a golf course on the other side of where the Jordan River normally flowed because his dad had taken him there once. With the increased width, the depth of the water and flow speed decreased as the flood spread out further. Rocking nearby, caught in a mangled tree, was somebody's green fiberglass canoe.

With some searching, he located an eight-foot pole and a broken piece of wood that widened at one end. The piece of wood might serve as a paddle if the water got too deep for the pole to push him across.

Besides getting knocked into the water by some floating ram, his primary concern ran down the middle of the river to 9000 South Street, or where the road would be if it wasn't inundated. A double line of electrical transmission poles dropped into the river valley across from where he stood and marched through the water to a flooded power substation about a half-mile downriver. The substation was completely underwater, but it occupied most of the width of the shallow valley, and he could see flood debris tangled in the mess of thick power cables that reached out of the water. While the transmission poles were moderately bent, the river level was just below the lowest west lines, and about mid-pole on the shorter east lines. To further complicate things, each transmission pole had six or more power lines strung between them. On each side of the poles, two or more lines swept down from one pole and up to the next at low, middle, and higher levels. The canoe should pass under the west lines, but the east lines posed more of a challenge. While electricity wouldn't be a threat, getting caught by the transmission lines between poles or tangled up in the mess at the substation would be a problem, especially since he had no hope of a rescue.

Nearly a mile east, he could see Interstate 15 between industrial buildings. The river water had flooded over the houses that bordered the golf course and lapped up to the edge of the buildings. His plan was to put in where the river was narrow, above the golf course, and try to cross as quickly as possible before he got carried too far downriver. If he were really lucky, he might get under and past the power lines quickly. Or at least make it beyond the river's midpoint to slower side flows before drifting into the mess at the substation.

He tucked the pole and board into the canoe and positioned the canoe on the bank to launch. After seating himself, he used the pole to push off and immediately questioned his sanity.

The mud-colored water betrayed the river's speed and turbulence. As soon as the canoe entered the water, it began to spin and bob. While he didn't expect to use the pole, the underwater currents made it difficult for him to pull the pole out of the water. By the time the pole was back in the canoe, the canoe was rapidly rotating into the center of the river.

He grabbed the makeshift paddle and used it to stop the rotation. Then, he repeatedly plunged it into the dirty froth to get some forward movement. He grimaced as slivers jabbed into his hands with the rough strokes. He easily ducked under the west power lines and scanned the fast-approaching east lines. The next transmission pole was also approaching. The lowest lines were buried beneath the water, but the mid-level set were dropping in and out of the water between poles.

The canoe passed over the first power lines of the mid-level set.

The canoe's front end started crossing the next lines of the mid-level, but the downriver drift was fast, and the rise of the cable quicker. He felt the canoe lift as it crossed the power line, and then the canoe's front dropped into the water. The churning water twisted the canoe over and spun it downriver. The twist bucked Chance into the water. He quickly surfaced and grabbed the flipped canoe. He was through the power lines, but he could see the growing chaos of flood-torn debris over the substation downstream.

A strong eddy shifted the canoe's direction and sent it spinning towards the east side of the river. Chance tried to flip the canoe but quickly gave up. Another current spun the canoe in the opposite direction, and he saw the mangled mess above the substation to the west. Straining to see where he was, he felt the water flow slow as he neared the east bank. Something bumped his legs and then his feet kicked what felt like a tree. He kicked towards the banks while using the canoe as a flotation aid. A concrete barrier that barely crested the water top appeared in his float path. Kicking hard, he felt the concrete scrape the back of the canoe as he passed over. A short distance downstream, the flooded river spread out comfortably for a distance before it narrowed again. From there, the river curved west and slowed as it seemed to gather its energy before it would rush through a narrow section.

Chance's feet kicked the river bottom. Struggling to stand, he staggered towards the bank, dragging the canoe. After pulling the canoe out of the water and stashing it near a leaning warehouse, he took a few minutes to remove the splinters from his hands. He was further downstream than he wanted, but he was on the right side of the river.

A breeze rustled the metal building, and Chance shivered. The sun was warm, but his clothes were soaked, and he felt exhausted. Above him, the sun moved lower westward. He wished he had a watch but supposed it didn't really matter what time it actually was.

He removed his pack, emptied its contents to dry, and added his shirt to dry as well. Then he sat down with his back against the metal warehouse wall, shielded from the wind but where he could still feel the warm sun. He drank one of the sports drinks and leaned his head back to rest.

———

Chance startled awake with the rattle of the building behind him as a small aftershock shook things for a few seconds. The sun hovered over the western mountains.

"I'm sorry I wasn't there for you, Cassie." His voice whispered, and his head dropped. "And I'm sorry I'm not there now. But I'm coming."

His pants were mostly dry, as were the items he had laid out. Feeling a little refreshed, he pulled the shirt back on, packed up, and headed south. His path wound through the shaken remains of industrial buildings and then stopped. In front of him, a wide waterway that began at the river on his right and stretched east past Interstate 15 replaced 9000 South Street. The mucky water didn't reveal whether the road had sunk or a fissure had opened. The waterway's rough edges—which started wide on the right and converged somewhere to the left, beyond the fragmented overpasses of the freeway—reminded him of a dirty zipper.

He briefly considered swimming across the calm water, but he had no desire to get wet again. With the distance less than a football field, he considered backtracking to get the canoe. He discarded both ideas when he realized that while the mall was south a few miles; it was also east.

A minute later he scrambled up the southbound off-ramp remains of Interstate 15. On his right, the freeway bridges over the 9000 South waterway were jagged protrusions. Thick, twisted and mangled rebar held firmly to shattered blocks of concrete. To the north and south, hundreds of vehicles sat abandoned on the fractured freeway. There were at least a dozen wrecks he could see, although most looked minor. About a block north, there were a handful of people examining some vehicles, and another group was further away. In the water on his right, he could see the outlines of several vehicles that had nose-dived when the bridges fell. From his raised position, he could see that the water ended about a mile away, just past the north-south running State Street.

Several minutes later, he walked by a large apartment complex. The lengthening shadows of the late afternoon exaggerated the cracked brick walls of the apartment buildings. Small groups of residents clustered in open spaces. Tents and tarps were set up and small cook fires burned.

Nestled between apartment buildings were the remains of a mobile home park. Few of the mobile homes were standing. Most had shaken and collapsed like houses made of cards, fallen in on their feeble stands with their walls and ceilings folded in.

At the street corner, a couple of restaurants and a pharmacy evidenced signs of looting.

A couple of blocks past State Street, the water gave way to broken asphalt on 9000 South. Chance turned south as the sun touched the western mountains. He passed a fire station on the right corner when a firefighter dressed in muddy turnouts exited.

The firefighter seemed surprised to see Chance. "Are you okay?" he asked.

The day's stress wanted to explode from Chance. "I'm good, but why aren't you guys out there? There're accidents on the freeway, fires…"

The firefighter held up a hand to stop Chance. "Whoa there, we want to help. Every firefighter and police officer I know would be out there if they could. But this is way worse than anything ever expected, planned for, or ever considered. We're doing all we can, but we're seriously limited. Our vehicles are stuck in the station with broken bay doors, and the station itself isn't actually safe. Even if we could get them out, none of our vehicles would get very far. The best we have are some ATVs. With the water lines out everywhere, we can't do much about any of the fires, even if we could get to them. Hospitals are running on limited reserve power or their emergency systems have failed. The few hospitals that still have some operational capacity are overwhelmed, understaffed, and running out of resources. We have a few small crews out, but we're limited to where we can walk. Since we can't do much, Chief asked us to check on our own families and then come back when they're taken care of. Some of the guys aren't married. I don't have kids, and my wife's okay. I need to get with my crew and head out. Do you need anything before I go? You look a little beat up."

"No, I'm good. I'm just trying to find my sister."

"Do you know where she's at?"

"The text I got before the quake yesterday said she was headed to the mall, so I'm guessing that's where she is."

"Wish we could help you, but as you know there are lots of others who are probably needing our help more. Just be careful. Things are getting bad. The cities in the area try to keep things looking good, but anyone who's been a first responder for any time knows there are some bad undercurrents in the valley."

"What do you mean?"

"Gang activity has been getting worse over the last decade. As well as drugs, homelessness, and shootings. Most of the public isn't aware of it, but we frequently encounter the remnants. And this kind of disaster...it's just going to amp things up. Wish I could tell you things will get better soon, but all our resources are at the breaking point. Don't expect outside help soon. The feds and outside agencies will try to come in, but it'll probably be close to a week before some aid can start trickling in. Even then, they won't be able to do much because of limited accessibility to the worst-hit areas. It'll be weeks before the least affected parts of the valley get electricity back and months before reliable water is restored. As for the hardest-hit areas, it could be a year or more before most of the area has much of a working infrastructure. And it'll be years before all the devastation is cleaned up and the Salt Lake Valley is back to normal."

"Thanks for the heads-up."

"No problem. Hope you find your sister safe."

The firefighter walked around the side and to the back of the building while Chance headed south. He glanced back when he heard the growl of ATV engines and saw three firefighters drive off, their ATVs loaded with equipment. Chance continued south and passed through a couple of neighborhoods where every house showed damage or destruction. Like the commercial buildings he'd gone by, the houses leaned, had busted windows, broken walls, and disfigured roofs. The evening sunlight reflected off the shattered solar panels on many roofs. Most of the panels had broken from their brackets and beaten against the shingled roofs.

He had walked for about five minutes when he realized how dark the sky was becoming. The sun had set, and twilight settled into the valley. A cool wind blew from the north, and clouds obscured the evening sky. Like the previous evening, it surprised him how dark it was getting. No streetlights. No building lights. No vehicle headlights. There was nothing to offset the rapid onset of night.

A droplet of water tapped his cheek, and he looked up. Dark clouds were gathering in the northwestern sky. He turned around and scanned the area for shelter.

Residential areas were closest, but many of the houses looked vertically challenged. He also didn't want to deal with any of the residents and questions that might arise.

In the next block, a large parking lot occupied the right side, and a grassy field was on the left. A school was set back behind the field, and he thought he could see a sheltered place. In the hastening darkness, he couldn't see any vehicles at the school.

The parking lot belonged to a popular entertainment complex with movie theatres, restaurants, and activities. Scores of cars were left in the ruptured lot. A man with a pack was trying to avoid five teenagers who were trying to surround him in the parking lot. The teens had bats and sticks with which they threatened the man. Several times the man attempted to back off, but each time the teens would cut him off.

Chance wanted to disappear to the school where it looked like he could avoid the situation in the parking lot, but he really disliked bullies, especially after the last month. He grabbed a couple of fist-sized rocks from the parking median and walked towards the group. "Hey, what's going on here?"

Chapter Nine

Help

T WO OF THE TEENS turned. One, a stocky boy with cropped, spiky blond hair, aimed his bat at Chance. "What do you want?"

"I want you to back off and leave this man alone."

"He has something we want."

"What?"

The boy grinned mischievously. "Whatever he has."

The second boy's head cocked. "Chance?"

"You know this guy?" the blond asked.

"Only that he was the star wide receiver for the Badgers. My old man was gushing about how good he was after our game against them last year. He made some crazy-good catches. Their team easily made the playoffs and won because of Chad's awesome throws and this guy's phenomenal skills. But earlier this year, Chance ratted out Chad and several of his teammates and got them suspended for several games. Might even have cost them the chance to go to state."

A glint flashed in the blond's eyes. "So, this is the guy Chad's been muttering about. Maybe we should take care of him for Chad."

Chance did not like where the conversation was headed. He didn't recognize the teens and could only guess they were locals who somehow knew Chad.

Hands tightened their grips on the bats and sticks. A bat swung at Chance's head, and he ducked left under the bat with a diagonal step that took him behind the blond. He grabbed the teen's shirt collar while his foot pressed against the heel and twisted right. The teen flailed backwards, and the bat whipped wildly back, hitting the second boy, who yelped and dropped his stick. Chance back-knuckled the base of the blond's skull, stunning him. Then he hurled a rock at the teen near the man.

The teen with the second bat swung at the man, who jumped back. A stick swiped through the air and streaked across the man's cheek. Before the third teen could do anything, the rock pummeled into his sternum. With his air knocked out, the stick dropped, and he staggered back clutching his waist.

Chance's second rock punched into his second opponent. Still behind the spiky blond, he twisted the bat from the teen's grip and stepped back.

The blond wobbled as he stood, his face pale in the rapidly fading light. "Let the old guy go. Get him!" He pointed at Chance.

Chance's bat blocked a swing from the other bat. He slid his bat down the teen's bat and across the boy's fingers. The boy yelped and dropped the bat. Chance slammed his bat's barrel end into his opponent's abdomen. The youth buckled over and crashed to the ground, gasping for air. The next teen's stick snapped against Chance's bat. Instead of waiting for the counterstrike, the teen quickly backed away.

The man picked up the fallen bat and stood near Chance. Of the five attackers, three were still recovering their ability to breathe, and their apparent leader was struggling to stay vertical.

"Anybody want any more?" Chance smiled at the surge of energy he felt.

"You'll regret this," the spiky blond teen spat. He backed away and motioned for the others to follow him towards the devastated entertainment complex.

When the teens disappeared into the night, the man turned to Chance. "Thanks for your help. My name's Dan."

"I'm Chance. Are you okay? It looks like that stick got your face good."

"It stings a bit. Probably should get it cleaned up before it gets infected." Dan looked at Chance. "Looks like you've got a few minor cuts and scrapes as well, although it doesn't look like they were from this encounter. Most people don't think too much about them, but remember this: in the type of disaster that's happened, you can't take any chances with any open wound. If it gets infected, you may be limited in how well you can treat it. And if the infection spreads, it could become sepsis, which can create widespread inflammation and even affect multiple organs. Severe sepsis can be difficult to treat with fully operational emergency care, but in our circumstances, without emergency care, it can be deadly."

Dan glanced around in the dark. "Do you know a safe place we can go? Preferably, someplace I can turn my light on without others seeing it."

"I'm just passing through, trying to find my sister. There's a school across the street that might have a less open place behind it. I can't imagine most kids wanting to take shelter at a school."

"Lead the way." Dan followed as Chance walked across and down the street to a light rail station where they wouldn't have to climb the fence. "So, Chance, do you know where your sister is?"

"I'm hoping she's at a mall about two miles south of here." Chance jumped down onto the buckled tracks and crossed over to the side of the light rail stop.

"Where's home?"

"It was a small community towards the southwest of the valley."

"Was?"

"After yesterday's big one, I walked home. I'd been at a lacrosse game earlier and was on my way home. I was supposed to take my sister, Cassie, to the mall. But she apparently got a ride about the time I left, but I didn't see the text until later. Our home, and the entire neighborhood, was destroyed and then probably got washed away in the flood."

"I heard about the flooding. Must've been devastating to watch."

"I was gone when the neighborhood got flooded. What about you? You seem like you're passing through as well."

"I am. I live a couple of hours south of here and came to Salt Lake for some consulting work. I was finishing dinner and about to head home when the quake struck."

"A couple of hours? I'm guessing you mean a couple of hours of driving. That's a long walk home."

"It would be, except," Dan paused, "I have some shortcuts ready in the Highland area which should cut my time down. Wait, what's that over there?"

Chance squinted in the dark to the left, where Dan was pointing. "Looks like a bunch of school buses. Probably the school district's transportation offices. I didn't see it before, probably because of the berm that was along the tracks after the houses."

"Let's go find a bus to stay in. They're probably less likely to be damaged than a building, and with that berm, unwanted visitors may not see us as easily." Dan motioned to the increasingly cloudy night sky. "Not to mention a bus might offer better protection from the rain that's coming."

They walked over to the transportation building. Unlike the dozens of buses, which were mostly damage free, the building's walls and windows were severely fragmented. After checking several buses, they found one that was unlocked. Water droplets pitter-pattered on the roof.

Dan retrieved a small light from his pack and stood it in a corner. He rummaged through the other contents while Chance pulled out his first aid kit, opened it, and felt relief to see everything had remained dry. He brought it over to Dan.

"I appreciate your willingness to use your own kit," Dan said as he pulled a zipped pouch from his pack, "but please save it for yourself or sister. We can use my kit to get my wound cleaned up. First, wash it out with this water." He handed Chance a small bottle.

Chance took the bottle and hesitated. "Are you sure? Clean water's in short supply."

"I've got a couple of water filters. And conveniently, we have this rain we can collect."

After rinsing the cut, Chance applied some antibiotic and a couple of butterfly bandages. Dan directed him to take an empty water bottle and place it under a stream of water off the corner of the busted roof of a nearby building.

When Chance returned, Dan had taken a small signal mirror from his pack to examine his cheek. "Not bad. Most people struggle to get the butterfly strips on right."

"Dad was in the army and was big on teaching us to be self-sufficient. He took Cassie and me backpacking and camping a lot."

"Well then, you might be familiar with this."

Dan removed a small backpacking stove from his pack and placed it in the aisle between bus seats. He prepared some water in a metal cup, boiled it on the stove, and then mixed it into a pouch. After a minute of cooling, he split it with Chance.

"Chicken teriyaki, backpacking style." Chance's nose twitched and his stomach growled its approval. "I've got a protein bar I can add."

Dan chuckled. "Keep your food. You'll probably need it to get home, or wherever you're going, after you find your sister." He removed a small pouch of dried apples and gave it to Chance. "You can take this. Don't worry about me. I've got what I need to get to where I'm going."

"You said you were in Salt Lake City. Was it really hit hard?"

Dan stopped chewing for a few seconds. The jaw shifted, and he swallowed. "The short answer is yes. Worse than anyone would've thought possible. I'm not a seismologist, but my guess is multiple ruptures were triggered, with each being way bigger than expected. Mother Nature has a way of surprising and reminding us we don't know as much as we think we do. I wasn't downtown, but it was easy to see the buildings weren't engineered for the hit they took. I found a safe spot to hole up in last night. When I left this morning, it looked like a war zone. I suspect that after the multiple aftershocks, much of the city will only be suitable for the wrecking ball. There were a few taller ones that collapsed, and others that are leaning so much I wouldn't want to be near them."

"What kind of consulting were you doing?"

"Security. Mostly IT-related, but also physical security. In a way, it's my job to help businesses be prepared for potential disasters."

"Which is why you were prepared."

"I always try to be prepared. You never know when your car will break down, a road closes, your flight gets canceled, or a disaster makes getting home challenging. Too many people have a normalcy bias and can't, won't, or don't want to see the chinks and holes in our society. There are too many things that can go wrong."

"Seems like a negative way to live."

Dan smiled warmly. "Depends on how you look at it. I like to prepare for the worst, hope for the best, learn from the past, look forward to the future, but live in and enjoy the present. Some say to pray to God as if everything depends on him, then work as if everything depends on you. If you're prepared, it actually makes it easier to enjoy life because you don't have a worry about what might go wrong. You know you can take care of it. It's those who aren't prepared who get thrown for a loop when life throws them a curveball."

Chance stifled a yawn. "Sorry, that was surprising. Guess I'm more tired than I thought."

"It's been a rough day. It might get a little chilly tonight. Do you have anything to keep warm?"

Chance pulled out his jacket. "Just this."

"That should be enough for tonight, especially in here. If it weren't cloudy and rainy right now, it'd likely get colder. The clouds that blew in looked more stratus, so the rain should be steady for a while. Maybe all night. Wet, but the clouds should keep the night a little warmer than a clear sky. I'll need to leave soon after sunrise. I expect to get to my destination well before tomorrow night, but I want to stack the deck in my favor."

Chance lay on the bus bench seat and stared at the ceiling, listening to the rain. "Do you have a family?"

"Yes. And they should be okay. At over eighty miles away, I'm sure it shook things. Might've broken some stuff. But everyone should be fine."

Another yawn broke Chance's determination to stay awake. "This bench is quite comfortable compared to the ground I slept on last night."

———

Chance woke to the smell of eggs. The night had been cool, but he was grateful for a dry place to sleep since the rain continued most of the night. A few more small aftershocks woke him, but the rain lulled him back to sleep. Grayish light was dawning through the clouds over the Wasatch Mountains. Dan offered him some of the scrambled eggs.

"They're not the best," Dan said as he mauled a bite of eggs, "only slightly better than rubber but at least they'll give you some energy."

"Thanks. I can't say I ever thought I'd be grateful for a school bus, but it wasn't too bad of a night."

"I suspect after a few days our little retreat here will be discovered, and more people will start sheltering in these buses."

Dan finished his eggs, tossed a small package of dried peaches to Chance, and then pulled out a camouflage tube that narrowed at one end. "This is a filter straw. It can screw onto the top of most regular water bottles, and you can drink the water. You can also put the end into water and sip. I have a few ways to filter and purify water. I want you to have this one. Without it, you risk serious illness, especially over the next few days."

Chance swallowed a dried peach. "Are you sure?" His hand reluctantly accepted the filter tube.

"Yes, keep it safe and use it." Dan packed up the few things he had out. "After you zonked out last night, I got thinking about what those kids were saying before and after you came by. You heard those kids wanting my pack. They didn't know what was in it, but you can see it would be helpful for anyone in these circumstances. Anyway, before you came by to help, those kids were talking about taking my pack back to Chad. From the conversation, it didn't seem like you knew them, but at least one knew who you were. And they all know a Chad, who I'm assuming you might know."

"Yes. I know him. And most of those he hangs out with. We played football together for several years."

"I don't need to know your history with him. Just to warn you. From their talk, it seems Chad might be at the mall. And he may have some sort of gang he's leading."

"Why would he be..." Chance thought for a moment. "He must've gone there after he talked to me, when I went home."

"If he's at the same mall as your sister, you need to be extra careful. Those guys last night didn't seem to mind taking things into their own hands. Everyone's gone a day with little or no law enforcement. Thousands are probably in need of help or rescue. I suspect many have done things they normally wouldn't consider, like taking food from a store."

A pang of guilt wrenched Chance when he realized he had done that, almost without thinking about what he was doing because he felt desperate.

"And in this increasingly lawless situation," Dan continued, "many people will end up doing things that will harm or even kill others if they feel like it's life or death. Today is the second day since the mega-quake. Everyone is under increased stress and pressure from the trauma. By tomorrow, hopelessness and increased fear will weave their way into the hearts of more people as the severity of this disaster twists into their consciousness, and expectations of rescue and recovery are shattered. With younger people, hormones always seem to amplify things. If Chad and his buddies are at the mall, you may be up against more than you can handle."

"Then I'd better get going." Chance grabbed his pack, stuffed the filter inside, and was at the bus door before he stopped. "Dan, thank you for sharing your food and for the water filter. If things are as bad as you say, Cassie will need my help."

"You're welcome, Chance, and good luck. I'll be heading out soon after I collect some more water. If you don't mind a final bit of advice, be cautious. Our world has changed, and it's become more dangerous. Hopefully, it's only temporary. You'll likely see the best and worst of what humanity offers."

Chapter Ten

Echoes from the Past

C HANCE FOLLOWED THE ROAD south, along the light rail tracks, until the road ended at a T-section. A footpath and bike trail paralleled the light rail tracks as they continued south. Chance had planned to turn west and head to State Street before going south again. But he decided there'd be less potential for unwanted contact with others if he continued south on the trail, away from commercial buildings.

After a few minutes along the trail, he slowed when he saw a high school football stadium. Bleachers leaned and fractures tore up the green playing surface. He crossed over where a tree had squashed a fence section and walked to midfield as if in a trance.

"Chance, are you aware of any illegal or unethical activity by any member of the team?"

The memory of the question made his insides squirm as much as it did when Vice Principal Barrett had asked it a month into his senior year. The follow-up statement did nothing to squelch the feeling.

"If you're aware of anything like cheating or hazing, or illegal activities, and don't report it, it would not only affect those involved but could jeopardize your standing on the team and your academics as you could be considered an accomplice or accessory to those violations."

Despite what spread across the school as fast as text messages could be sent, he had not been the one to first report cheating, hazing, and the use of alcohol by members of the football team. He knew what his teammates would likely face if he told the truth. But he also knew he would disappoint himself and his parents if he lied, and if the truth came out after he lied, it would be much worse for him. So, with reluctance, he related what he had seen and heard.

Since middle school, Chad had become obsessed with becoming the best quarterback. As freshmen, his grades suffered, and he and some of his buddies coerced some academic help. After they joined the varsity team as juniors, Chad's obsession snowballed, and the help he acquired on assignments turned into more "specialized tutoring," as they called it, including some elaborate cheating schemes. He also started bullying younger players. He hadn't started the hazing, but he certainly perpetuated and increased it. Regarding the alcohol accusations, since their junior year, Chance had his suspicions and heard stories, but he knew nothing for certain because he started getting involved with other sports and limited how much he hung out with Chad and most of the football team.

A week after his report, Chad and ten members of the team were suspended from playing for three games. Several others had warnings. Chance was surprised the suspension wasn't longer until he heard rumors that Chad's dad had pulled some financial strings to influence the outcome. The team had been on a winning streak towards securing a spot in the state championship playoffs, but with the star quarterback and several key players suspended, that option didn't look good.

Immediately, Chance's social life dropped off a cliff. He became singled out, and everyone seemed to know him, but not in a good way. His phone was flooded with bluejacked, demeaning texts, and his meager social media accounts were inundated with hateful posts.

He played in the next three football games, the last of which was in the same stadium he was standing in. Each time, he pulled the team to a win. Their defense was good, but the offensive line was lacking without the suspended players. The other quarterbacks weren't even close to Chad's skill, and Chance was challenged in completing plays. After each win, the bullying, intimidation, and hate continued.

Then Chance got called into Vice Principal Barrett's office again. Barrett looked embarrassed and almost as if he was being forced to do something he didn't agree with, but he didn't say as much. Instead, Chance was informed that he would be suspended for two games on suspicion of cheating in classes. He almost blew up in protest with his exclamation that he had never cheated on anything. Barrett was very apologetic as he explained that the school was being extra cautious in the face of recent events, but that three students had gone to the principal claiming to have seen Chance cheating on a test. Barret explained to Chance that there was no proof of cheating, only the word of the three students, and their accounts, when questioned individually, were suspicious. Chance asked who the students were and was told the names and their reports were confidential. After he left the office, he saw the self-satisfied looks from several football players as he passed them in the hall.

The team lost its next game. It wasn't even close. Chad performed well enough, but the offense struggled and was defeated by the better defense of their opponent.

Another loss followed. Chad became even more furious with Chance. The bullying online and at school went up several notches.

Chance couldn't play in the next game because he got sick. The team lost again. Chance missed several practices because of the illness. He blamed the sickness on the stress. Chad didn't believe him, which meant nobody else believed him. And to be honest with himself, Chance was relieved he had a good excuse, even if it resulted in more bullying. He would've quit the team, but he didn't feel right about giving up. By this point, he had stopped using social media and seldom looked at his phone.

The past week was a bye week. He'd gone to practice, but his heart wasn't in it. When asked, he excused himself by saying he was still recovering from the illness. Chad's fury almost got them both kicked out of practice.

If the earthquake hadn't struck, the following week would have been the last game of the regular season, and a win would have gotten them to the state championship.

But that future was no longer.

A cool wind blasted Chance from the north, waking him from his thoughts and memory.

Was telling the truth worth it, he wondered. It had only resulted in misery, and now the future was completely uncertain. The last several weeks had been the worst he'd ever had. The only friends who hadn't shunned him were a few on the cross country and lacrosse teams, players who didn't care about football.

He knew Chad would carry out his threats against Cassie. Being a freshman did little to protect her, and she had already received some bullying because of what Chance was accused of.

His dad had said little about it, except something about telling the truth would be best in the long run.

Chad was right about one thing: Chance's dad thought football was a man's sport. Other sports were okay to watch, but only when football wasn't an option. Like Chance, his dad was a wide receiver in high school and then played in college, so he always wanted to watch Chance play.

And his dad hadn't come to any of Chance's cross country meets and seldom went to lacrosse games. Chance didn't blame him though as he often worked when games occurred, and watching people run long distances wasn't very interesting. Chance liked to run, so he did it more for himself, and he discovered with some coaching that he was actually quite good at it as well.

Chance shivered and looked east. The sun was rising over the mountains. He wasn't certain, and hadn't noticed it before, but the mountains seemed a little different. The night's rain in the valley had dusted the mountains with snow, but the tops and sides weren't the same, like several large landslides had scoured the mountain range. He was certain that some ridgelines were different. Below the snow-dusted tops, autumn reds and yellows were making their way down from the higher elevations.

He turned and looked back across the field, still not knowing if he'd done the right thing in telling the truth about Chad and the other players, but he knew what he needed to do now. He needed to find his sister and get them both to safety. His gaze shifted to the southwest, where he knew the mall was about a mile away, and saw a dense mass of smoke surging upwards.

Chapter Eleven

Smoke Signals

CHANCE SPRINTED WEST ACROSS the field towards State Street. His pace slowed as he turned south and passed the high school buildings on the left and a neighborhood to the right. He crossed over where State intersected an east-west road. An expansive commercial plaza occupied the southwest corner with several professional offices and restaurants. As with every other place he'd seen, abandoned vehicles littered roads and parking lots when their occupants realized they could drive nowhere because of the severely damaged roads.

Behind the business plaza, the black plume of smoke rose from a large retail store. Flames spat from the front doors and whipped above the rooftop. Groups of people clustered around the parking lot, most watching the building burn. Between State Street and the parking lot, a broken sidewalk wound through a tree-filled park-like strip.

Chance kept on the quake-damaged road, using the trees to separate himself from those in the parking lot. The tree-covered park strip continued along the parking lot past the south end of the burning store, where the remains of a restaurant smoldered at one corner of the south end. The treed park wrapped behind the restaurant's remains, and Chance could glimpse the mall through the foliage.

Part of Chance wanted to burst into a run and get to the mall as quickly as possible, but Dan's warning came to mind. Instead, he used the tree cover to approach the north end of the mall's parking lot and observe.

The first thing he noticed was vehicle chaos. It was like the drivers had panicked and tried to leave either during or after the quake. Some cars had dropped into the shallow fissures that splintered and cracked the asphalt. Others were high-centered on blacktop that had erupted upwards. There weren't as many vehicles as he thought there should be, and he wondered if some had left. A few people wandered through the cars along the lot's outer perimeter. Chance doubted most were there for good reasons. All the light poles were bent, and some had fallen to the ground.

The mall looked fragmented. Splits tore through walls. Store facades had collapsed. Decorative trimmings were ripped from their places and lay crumpled on the ground. The raised entranceway over the east anchor store lay demolished, completely burying the main doors. On the roof, fragments of pyramid and cone-shaped skylights jutted their fractured remains skyward. The wall's partial collapse had crushed the truck delivery doors inward on the side of the anchor store.

The treed strip continued to wrap the north edge of the mall's parking lot, with a few streets breaking through to the north neighborhood. Uncertain of what he might encounter inside the mall, Chance warily walked through the trees along the north while scanning the mall. From the northernmost point, he could see the tattered remains of Interstate 15 across the parking lot to the west. A large flock of California seagulls circled lazily beyond the freeway, and he wondered if the river was still swollen beyond flood stage. A lone building, an outdoor recreation store, stood precariously near the freeway. The north anchor store of the mall was directly south of him, and he could see the damaged but still accessible entrance. The tree cover ended where he stood, but from his vantage point, the rest of the mall evidenced similar or worse damage to what he'd already witnessed.

He scratched his left temple as he studied the building. Blocked windows and doors obscured and hid the interior of the mall. The few places that allowed a glimpse inside only revealed darkness. The sun on his left approached midmorning.

A fleck of light on the rooftop caught his attention. Someone crouched and shifted to another location near the corner. Chance began methodically scanning the roof and identified two other individuals, all of whom appeared to be watching. Dan's warning replayed through his mind. Were they waiting for him, he thought, or just keeping guard? His plan to come to the mall, find Cassie, and get them to safety suddenly felt...lacking. He had never considered the possibility of anyone stopping him.

His eyes dived into the mall with more scrutiny. The various entrances were all damaged. However, only a few seemed inaccessible because of the earthquakes. Most looked strategically blocked.

Between the expansive parking lot that acted almost like an asphalt moat and the barricaded entrances, getting inside unseen would not be a simple task. He was not very familiar with the layout of the mall, but he wished he remembered the stores Cassie liked to frequent and where she might be. And who else was at the mall? Was it just Chad and his minions, or were other people stuck inside as well?

A rifle shot blasted across the parking lot from the east. Chance saw a small group of people hastily retreat from the mall.

He retreated into the trees and returned east, back to where he had started. From there he went back to State, and then south where the shaken remains of a few restaurants helped conceal him as he continued south nearly three blocks. A couple of strips of trees lined the mall's southeast access road, and he cautiously used them to approach the southeast corner. While not fully protected, his scouting showed this approach yielded the best cover right up to the mall.

Between points of cover, he took a few moments to scan the roof edge and along the building. As he entered the final grass and tree strip that led right up to the mall's southeast corner, his hope of reaching the mall unseen increased. Besides a thick section of bushes and trees, the strip sloped away and provided additional cover as he neared the south side. He passed three truck delivery doors that were closed, bent, and locked. A nearby solid metal door was also locked.

He skirted along the base of the anchor store's wall towards the south doors. Unlike other entrances, this one was only partially obstructed. Almost all the glass in the doors and windows had shattered.

His heart pumped wildly as he stepped over the glass and first set of doors. More broken glass, pieces of the ceiling, and other debris littered the floor of the store's entry. Light from the entrance spilled reluctantly onto the first floor of the department store. He wondered why the entrance wasn't barricaded if the mall was under lockdown. Or, the thought occurred to him, maybe the gated entrance from the store into the main mall was locked. He remembered most stores had gates that could close and prevent access, which might be simpler than trying to block a full entrance.

He moved through the toppled shelves, displays, and spilled inventory. Light became fleeting. His sight adjusted to the dimness as he navigated the quake-ravaged store. The store to mall security gate came into view, backlit by beams of light that pierced down from high above. He listened for a minute and then warily tried, and failed, to open the gate. Beyond the gate, he could see the railing of the second floor wrap around, leaving an opening down to the ground level. Shards of skylights opened to the sky above, where sunlight streamed through. Above him was the landing for the department store's second floor.

Chance turned back into the darkness. It took a minute for his eyes to readjust after being exposed to the streamers of sunlight. He picked his way around the tossed inventory and broken shelves and silently moved towards the escalator that appeared to lean in the low light.

The treads of the escalator felt uneven under his feet as he ascended to the second floor. Glass shattered, piercing the silent store. He froze at the top step and waited, his exhale caught momentarily. The quiet weighed on him like an ominous shadow. From the left, beyond piles of night that were strewn across the floor, trickles of light passed through the closed gate. In the near dark he could make out a cluttered path from the escalator to the gate. His ears strained to hear something, anything. From the main mall, distant, muffled voices filtered in. He hoped to recognize Cassie's, but the whisper-soft sounds disappeared. Inside his chest, the thump of his heart seemed to increase with each step towards the gate. A short distance beyond the closed gate, the second floor broke away before the sunlight that seemed to drip from the tattered skylights.

"Good to see you, Chance. I started doubting you'd come until some buddies saw you last night. Sure took your time getting here. Or maybe you just needed to work up your pathetic courage to finally come in."

Chapter Twelve

Ambushed

C HANCE WHIPPED AROUND. CHAD and six of his buddies stood in a half-circle like shadow statues in the partial darkness. Chance's eyes darted around, looking for an escape. The closed gate behind him confirmed his lack of options.

"What do you want, Chad?"

"What do I want? How about you? I'll bet I can guess what you want. But don't worry about Cassie. We've been taking good care of her and her friends, and made sure they aren't running about getting into trouble or getting hurt. You should thank us for doing your job in babysitting your sister."

"You'd better not have hurt her, or her friends."

"Or what? Are you going to report us to the principal? What about the police? Maybe you should just call them and make things easier for when things get too dirty for your liking."

"I wasn't the one who first reported you guys."

"You weren't? That's hard to believe when my sources say otherwise. So self-righteous Chance is a liar."

A few rough chuckles came from the surrounding shadows.

"Your sources probably wouldn't know the truth if it bit them. Vice principal Barrett asked me if I knew of actions that were illegal or against school policy. He said someone else had reported them but asked me what I knew."

"So, there we have it, confirmation from the donkey's mouth. I'd use another word for you, Chance, but I know your poor, tender ears can't handle it."

The shadows laughed.

"Chance decided he should just turn his back on his teammates and rat us out," Chad continued. "Even though we only did what was best for the team and our school. You took my life from me. I had scouts coming to watch, and because of you I didn't play. And because of you, my chances of any kind of football scholarship are nil, and our team won't get the chance to win the state championship."

"Are you serious, Chad? You're blaming me for your bad choices? And for an earthquake that shattered our world? You have a twisted sense of what's right."

"You're the one who's twisted. I don't know what happened to you. What happened to our dreams of winning state, playing college ball, and going pro? I never lost sight of them, but somewhere you did."

Chance could feel the agitation building in Chad's voice and sensed the shift in the others. "Just let me get Cassie and we'll leave. I'll even quit the team so you never have to deal with me again."

"That's where you're wrong." The edge of Chad's voice sharpened. "Unfortunately, the last few games proved that without you we have little chance of going to state, even with my superior skills. Which meant," his voice soured, "I needed you on the team. But since the state championships aren't happening now, you're no longer needed, and we can deal with you for the last time. You won't ever have to worry about football dreams again."

Chance stepped back and felt a light clank of the gate against his heel. Six shadows inched towards him.

"Don't make it too fast, guys," Chad said. "And, Chance, don't worry about your sister. We've been waiting to deal with her and her friends until after you're taken care of."

The right arm of each shadow lifted into view and extended. It took half a second for Chance to realize the extensions were bats that had been too low before and obscured by the shadows of destruction behind the group. Chad hung back while the six warily stepped forward. It took another second for Chance to understand why they didn't all attack; they didn't want to get hit by someone else's bat in the low light.

The forms of his opponents increased in clarity as his eyes became more adjusted to the dark, and he recognized Blaze, Rocco, Jax, Axel, Knox, and Slade. He could imagine drool from their excited grins as bats raised on approach.

His pulse jumped, and he ducked under Slade's wild swing. Slade's bat clashed into the gate as Chance stood behind Slade's right shoulder. Knox over-corrected for the duck, pulled in the swing, and accidentally smashed his bat into Slade. Chance grabbed Slade's collar and pressed his right foot into Slade's calf. Off balance, Slade started falling back when Knox's bat knocked his breath out.

Chance snatched the bat from Slade's relaxed grip in a reverse hold, folded it under his forearm, and slammed its barrel end directly behind him into Knox. Knox doubled over, gasping for air.

Axel's bat flew at Chance in a wide horizontal swing. Chance lifted his arm, the bat still laid back against his forearm, and blocked. His arm buzzed under the impact. He grabbed his bat with his left hand and arced it into Axel's. Instinctively, he dodged back from several blurs that came at him from the left.

His eyes skipped around the room. The near darkness and piles of debris made mapping an escape route challenging. Chad had disappeared into the shadows.

Rocco's bat swung down. Chance's bat raised and blocked. Jax's bat slammed into the back of Chance's right thigh, and he felt his leg go numb. Chance hobbled back and tripped over Knox.

Knox and Slade, each still gasping for breath, tried to wrestle Chance to the floor, but their lack of air made their attempts feeble. Chance's feet wasted no time kicking their faces.

Chance's left hand still gripped his bat while his right picked up a second bat from the floor. He switched to a reverse grip with the left bat and raised it to block another wild swing. His right bat swung low and smashed into Jax's left calf. Jax howled as his leg gave way and dropped him to the floor.

Chance scooted back into the store as he stood. Blaze and Rocco maneuvered towards him. Axel was regaining his breath. The other three were out for the moment. He took another step back, and a powerful blow smashed into his upper right arm. Searing pain tore through the arm's nerves, and the instant numbness caused the bat to release. He wobbled left and saw Chad smiling at him.

"Chancy, I don't think you're letting our guys have any fun. And now you're wanting to leave our party when things are just getting interesting."

Chance stepped back towards the store's wall as Chad's slow advance pressed on him to retreat. Blaze and Rocco moved to Chad's sides and spread out to keep him from escaping. He could almost feel the wall behind him and the fallen display shelves on the right like ominous unseen obstacles. He almost missed Rocco's swing, but his left hand raised the bat-shield.

CRACK!

His arm vibrated from the impact. The bat snapped above the taper, and the barrel end dropped to the ground.

"Before I let our buddies Rocco and Blaze have fun with you, I just wanted to let you know I really considered giving you more of a sporting chance. But considering you didn't give us a chance and just threw us under the bus, we're going to return the favor."

Chance dive rolled to the right. He didn't know what he was diving into, only that it was probably better than whatever his attackers had in mind. His head knocked something onto the floor when he dived, and his pack provided some cushion as he rolled over the collapsed display.

"After him!"

On the floor, he quickly took his bearings, glancing around. The darkness on his right was the wall. In front were more displays or shelves. To his left, near the center of the store, a faint aura of light seemed to come up from the floor. *The escalators*, he thought. From his position near the floor, he could also see there was very little that might trip him if he could run straight.

His former teammates were coming around the toppled displays when he took off in a sprint towards the store's center. He slowed in time to avoid a collision with the cracked glass railing that circled the two nonfunctional escalators. Behind him, Blaze, sped through the dimness, closing in on his target. Chance grabbed the top rail, looked down into a near abyss, and swung himself over. His feet thudded unevenly on the escalator treads, and his left ankle complained loudly. Clenching his jaw, he almost leaped the rest of the way down. Glass shattered above and rained down on the escalator. Chance scrambled through the debris field of the ground floor, sped on by his adrenaline and dark-adjusted eyesight, and dodged through the doors into the bright daylight. Shielding his eyes, he turned left and launched into a sprint. Behind him, he heard a gunshot as he crossed State Street. Across the street, he entered the parking lot of a shopping plaza and turned left again to head north to the other end of the lot where he collapsed between some parked cars outside of a quake-scarred restaurant.

After a minute, his pulse and breathing slowed. A couple of minutes passed, and the burning in his lungs subsided. He leaned back against the car and looked up into the sky. Nearby, he heard some voices talking and getting closer. His heart quickened for a minute.

"Are you sure they're in there?" a baritone voice asked.

A second male responded. "Would I lie about this? I'm telling you, there were three teenage girls who went inside, all alone. They were trying to be sneaky. Probably hoping to find something to eat. Nobody else is around, and there ain't no cops to stop us. There's three of us and three of them. Let's go in and pay them a visit."

Chapter Thirteen

Allies in Ashes

W HAT THEY MEANT BY paying the girls a visit, Chance guessed would be nothing nice. The voices sounded like they were a few cars away and headed towards the restaurant near him. He dipped his head to look under the cars and saw three pairs of shoes walking toward the restaurant front. His right arm throbbed. The ache in the ankle he twisted from the awkward escalator landing had lessened. His right thigh was numb. A warm throbbing on his head told him a bump was forming. He wanted a hot tub to soak out the soreness, and then to sleep in his bed all night.

His bed. The thought reminded him he had no bed. No home. Nothing. His SUV couldn't even be used. Everything he owned he had with him, or maybe in the SUV if it wasn't looted. He hoped his dad had survived, but he really didn't know and didn't know how to find out. At least he still had Cassie.

Cassie! Chance realized that Chad actually gave him some hope. His sister was alive and supposedly somewhere in the mall. For nearly two full days, he hadn't really known. He hoped she was alive and that he'd find her at the mall. But until his encounter with Chad, he hadn't known.

"You two ready?" The voice, a quiet rasp, came from the corner of the restaurant.

Chance really wanted to just leave and feign innocence of anything that might be about to happen. *Maybe they're friends who are giving the girls a surprise*, he reasoned. Deep inside, he knew what they wanted wasn't good. He'd heard similar lust-filled braggarts in locker rooms. Guys who treated girls as trophies and gave them no respect. He figured none of them had younger sisters and probably didn't have dads who drilled respect for others into them.

He risked a glance around the front bumper. The backs of the men disappeared around the corner. From his brief glimpse, they looked college age, and he thought they'd be right at home in a party-oriented fraternity. Based on their dirty clothes, he guessed they had gone out for an evening of fun when the Big One struck.

His head shook at himself, knowing what he needed to do. He mentally inventoried what he had. Basically nothing except a gun, and he didn't want to use that unless things became extreme, as someone would likely get seriously hurt or killed. He wished he had his lacrosse stick.

A girl's scream broke through the fractured restaurant walls.

In about five seconds, Chance rushed to the restaurant's shattered door and walked in.

One man, a stocky man with short dark hair, had tightly gripped the forearms of a young woman with long blonde hair. The other two girls, one with short dark brown hair and the other a shoulder-length brunette, huddled close together as they backed past the counter into the food preparation area. Two men actively prevented the girls' escape, almost like wolves herding prey.

"Are you open for business?" Chance asked.

A man with dirty blond, short hair, one of the two herding the girls, turned and glared. "Beat it, kid."

The other herder, a tall, dark-haired man who looked like he'd be at home on a football team's defense, added, "Yeah, if you know what's good for you, you'd leave now."

The fear-filled blue eyes of the blond held in the man's grip burned into Chance. His eyes narrowed. "I don't think these nice young ladies want to serve you three, so I suggest you'd better take your business elsewhere."

A smirk shot at Chance from the dirty blond. "You're goin' wish you'd left, boy. Girls, don't bother leaving. We've already been through this place before, and the front entrance is the only working door. The few windows have broken glass that'll rip you apart. We'll take care of you after we take care of some unwanted business."

The three men turned and sauntered towards Chance, certain of the outcome. Chance's heart raced as he shifted left and moved around strewn tables, chairs, and pieces of ceiling. His brain shifted into high gear as he surveyed the area. The dark blond closed in on the left while the other two approached from center right, cutting off any hope of escape out the door. The blond-haired girl hid with her friends behind the counter.

Chance thought about the gun in his pack, wondering if he should have gotten it out before but realizing there wasn't time now. His eyes continued scanning for options while they warily watched his soon-to-be attackers. The men, while eager to teach him a lesson, also seemed cautious, as if uncertain what to expect from a teenager who stood up to them. He guessed they had never encountered anyone younger who didn't cave to their demands.

From his left peripheral view, Chance watched Blondie close the distance while he also monitored the other two men. Blondie launched a right wild hook. Chance twisted slightly left, raised his left arm, caught the hook under it, and clamped his arm down over the hook. At almost the same time his right leg stepped behind Blondie's left hip, while his right arm crossed the chest. A quick pivot on his right foot, while sweeping the left behind, sent the dark blond man flying over his hip.

The throw smashed Blondie into a leaning table and silenced his yelp with a thud. A long metal tube, twisted at one end, rolled out from under the table. Chance snatched up the broken table leg and faced his other two opponents. The two men paused, and each pulled out a knife before resuming their approach.

With the men's backs towards the single exit, Chance yelled to the girls. "Get out!" He backed around the room as the knives snapped at him like starving raptors. Behind the men, the girls ran to the door, but the stocky, dark-haired man detached himself from the melee and cut off the girls' escape, forcing them to retreat to the counter.

The tall dark's blade thrust towards Chance's abdomen. He swiped the tube down in an arc and caught the man's wrist. The tube's twisted end yanked across the wrist and threw the knife across the room. The man backed off as he voiced a string of colorful metaphors. Then, the end of the tube slammed into stomach and he dropped to the floor, struggling for air.

Chance backed to the counter, towards the end away from the girls. The stocky, dark-haired man was more cautious than his friends. The knife hissed in front of him like a snake trying to determine where to strike. He feinted a thrust, and Chance's parry missed as the knife pulled back. The man's arm swept around and snapped down on Chance's back.

Chance stumbled forward and swept the tube upwards into the man's sensitive zone. He felt only a little guilty about the cheap shot when the man doubled over and slammed his head against the counter's edge. But he remembered his dad had always warned him there were no rules in a street fight.

Glancing over at the girls, he motioned them towards the door. "They're down. Get out!" Not seeing the knife in the man's hand, he looked behind him and saw the knife extending from his backpack. He reached over his shoulder to remove the blade, but it wouldn't release its hold.

The three teenagers darted out the door as the dark blond man struggled and pushed himself up. He reached behind his back and retrieved a handgun, which he pointed at Chance across the restaurant.

Bang!

A bullet whizzed past Chance and sparked against metal in the food preparation area. He ducked behind the counter, and two more shots ricocheted behind him. Behind him, the sound of a thick liquid throbbed out of a hole and began puddling onto the floor. The odor of over-used oil assaulted his nose.

Chance risked a glance over the counter.

"Get up!" Blondie shouted at the taller man, who was still struggling for air. "He's trapped in the kitchen area, and the girls just left. Take care of him and maybe we can still get the girls."

Chance eyed the door. He'd be an easy target if he tried to run now, but maybe he could draw them into the kitchen area and get around them. The stocky man lay crumpled on the floor at the end of the counter, whimpering and moaning. He figured the stocky guy would probably be out for a few minutes. The tall guy's breathing was under control, and he stood by his buddy with a knife in hand. Blondie's eyes looked possessed as they scoured the counter and kitchen area.

Chance ducked as another couple of shots flew overhead. Without looking at his adversaries, he sprinted back into the kitchen area and dove behind another counter.

More shots chased after him. His feet slipped. Looking down, he saw a glossy puddle spreading from a nearby appliance where oil dripped in thick glops onto the floor. Several heavy-duty round pans lay scattered across the floor. He grabbed several of the pans and dodged further back into the kitchen. Blondie and the tall man had passed the counter and were splitting up to cut him off.

Another angry shot tore through the kitchen.

"Boy, your failure to leave is going to cost you." Blondie's agitated voice reverberated off the broken walls and cooking equipment. He fired a round into the back of the kitchen.

Chance watched from a lower position. Blondie was moving into the kitchen on his left while the tall one came along the right side. He cupped his hands and spoke to the wall on the left. "You keep missing. But I'm guessing that's the story of your life."

Several bullets ripped into the appliances and equipment.

Chance scooted around the end of the preparation counter and stood to face the tall guy who was a short distance away at the other end of the counter.

"Hey!" was all the tall man could say before Chance had sent a pan flying at his face like a heavy-duty flying disc. The man's head jerked back and his eyes rolled as the body froze for a second and then dropped to the floor.

Chance dropped low, moved over to the fallen man, and took his knife. A sound came from behind him, from where he had just come. He dove right behind the end of the counter as Blondie aimed.

Bang! Click.

Letting loose a profanity, Blondie released the ammunition magazine and fished in his pockets. Chance whipped a pan through the air.

Blondie sidestepped the attack as he pulled out another magazine, slammed it into the gun, and pulled back the action to load. His aim was cut short with the impact of another spinning pan, and he fired two rounds into the cooking appliances.

Chance snatched the pan lying on the floor by the tall guy and sent it spinning at the dark blond. The heavy pan smashed into the collarbone, and the man sputtered a cough, followed by heaves of desperate breaths.

Hamburgers? Thought Chance. *Is that what I'm smelling?* He pivoted around and saw tongues of fire dancing across a griddle top, following a line of oil that meandered across and spilled onto the floor. A tiny flame dancer dove off the edge and, flickering orange-red, burst from the other side of the kitchen. He moved when something grabbed his ankle.

"Got you now, you punk kid." The tall man was still lying on the floor, but he had recovered enough to grab Chance.

Chance kicked free. "Dude, a fire's started. Get out!"

The man's eyes widened as his nose registered the truth of Chance's words.

At one end of the front counter, the stocky man used the counter for help in standing. His face blanched when he registered the fire.

Chance darted around the opposite end of the counter and sped to the door. He glanced back at the kitchen. The fire had grown and spread quickly. The flames were licking up the wall and lapping at the ceiling. Thick smoke filled the restaurant. Through the smoke he heard coughing and saw murky shadows of three individuals. He escaped through the door and ran east, where he took refuge inside a sports store. Inside, he positioned himself near the busted front windows where he could watch outside.

Dark smoke billowed from the cracked walls and windows of the restaurant. Through the broken windows, black-tinged flames angrily gyrated inside. One after another, three figures pushed through the doorway and crawled out. They continued north, distancing themselves from the burning restaurant, slowed only by continuous coughing.

Something moved behind Chance. He spun around. In the shadows of the store were five figures, two standing and three crouched, watching him.

Chapter Fourteen

The Mall Fortress

IT TOOK A MOMENT for Chance's eyes to adjust after staring out in the sunlight. One of the crouched figures stood, and he recognized her as the shoulder-length brunette from the restaurant. "I'm glad you guys got out," he said.

"Thanks to you. Looks like you burned the place." She paused as she watched outside for a few seconds. "Too bad those guys aren't burning with it." She took a step towards Chance, paused a moment and then added. "Thanks again for your help. I'm Tori. These are my friends, Maya and Ava."

The two crouching figures stood and joined Tori. Chance started to ask about the other two and then realized the already-standing figures were mannequins. "I'm Chance. I'm surprised those two are still standing."

"They weren't. We stood them up and dressed them up better, along with some others, to throw people off. Most people are looking for food, so they're not likely to come in. There have been a few who have seemed to back off when they saw the mannequins."

"So, you're not from this area."

Tori's face lowered. "We don't live far away. Mostly we use this for staging, and to make sure we're not followed when we find something to take home. Although there's not much of anyone's homes left."

"What about your parents?"

Tori huffed. "I can take care of myself."

"None of us were home when the big earthquake happened. Neither were any of our parents," Maya said. Her blond hair shook briefly when she added, "We don't know where they are or if they're okay."

"The quake destroyed my home, and the entire neighborhood. Then the river flooded, and I think everything got washed away. I wasn't home during any of it. Dad was working near Salt Lake, and I haven't heard anything from him either."

"A flood?" asked Tori. "You must live by the river. I heard it flooded really bad but haven't seen it."

"Yeah, it did. I lived about six miles south of here."

"So, why are you up here?"

"My sister went to the mall with some friends. I was supposed to take her, but I was late from a lacrosse game. She texted me soon after I left that she'd gotten a ride with a friend, but I didn't see the text until later. I found out a little while ago that she is at the mall, but—". His words dropped off, wondering how to explain what had happened.

"But the mall's been taken over by a gang," Tori continued.

"Yeah, you could say that. How'd you know?"

Tori's shoulder's shrugged. "Anyone who's been around here for the last day and a half knows that. Some psychos patrol the roof and shoot at people who try to get near. We were shot at yesterday. Inside the gang has control of everything. If your sister's still inside, she's probably a hostage."

"I wouldn't have put Chad as a gang leader, but I guess he kinda is. Definitely not someone to get on the wrong side of."

"Chad? You know the gang leader?"

"Yeah. We played on the same football team for years. He's an amazing quarterback, but over the past year I've learned he's not a nice guy."

"I'm guessing you two aren't on good terms anymore."

Casey's brow furrowed. "Not even close. Before the restaurant incident, I'd gotten to the end store of the mall. He and some of his goons ambushed me. I'm sure they would've killed me or at least injured me so badly I would've wished to be dead. But at least I found out Cassie is there."

Tori turned to her friends. "See, he's not like most guys. Probably because he has a little sister."

"How do you know she's his *little* sister?" Eva asked.

"If she weren't, she would've driven herself."

Chance nodded. "Yes, she's a couple of years younger."

Tori's eyes shifted upwards, as if remembering something. "Do you know where Cassie is in the mall?"

"No. If I knew where she liked to go in the mall, I'd guess there. But I don't. And even if I did, if she's a hostage, Chad's guys would've taken her where it was more secure."

"I think I could help." Tori's brown eyes narrowed on Chance.

"What!?" Maya said. "You want to go back there?"

"We owe him," added Tori, "but, more specifically, I can help. If we can get into the shop at the lower end, there's a service tunnel that might get us inside."

"Are you referring to the loading delivery doors at the south end?" Chance asked.

"Yep. It was a mall service shop. I know someone who worked there for a long time. A few times I got to wander with him through the service tunnels. A few years ago, the mall shut the shop down and contracted most of the mall maintenance out to other companies."

"Do you think the service tunnel is still open?"

"Yeah, if the quake didn't damage it too badly, most of the tunnels are probably still usable. Only the maintenance shop was shut down. The service tunnels are, or were, still used for accessing utility systems and some storage areas by maintenance and mall personnel."

Chance scanned the store and squinted towards the back. "I'll need to scout things out better, both on the outside and more particularly on the inside." He squinted toward the back of the store. "I'm going to borrow some binoculars to help scout the outside. If those tunnels are usable, hopefully I can use them to figure out where Cassie is."

"We. I'm going with you. Maya and Ava," Tori turned to her friends. "You should probably just go home. Chance, while we can check out the outside easily enough, it'd probably be safer and easier to go inside after dark. As you probably saw, there isn't much cover getting to the mall, so night should make us less obvious."

"I appreciate your willingness to help, but I need to go in alone."

"Why? So you can show off your bravado? It's been a few years, but I've been in the service tunnels, unlike you."

Chance's head shook. "Chad and his goons aren't guys to mess with. If they're stooping low enough to take my sister and her friends captive, and shooting at people who come near the mall, they won't hesitate to hurt you."

Tori's brown eyes softened. "It's nice that you care, but how do you plan to take on all of them on your own?"

"Hopefully, I won't have to take them all on at the same time."

"You know that hope isn't a good plan. Right?"

"Look, I could use your help to scout out the perimeter and then to get inside. But once I'm in, it'd be safer for you not to be there."

"I may look like a helpless girl, but today wasn't the first time I've encountered guys who want to take advantage of me. Those brutes caught me off guard. I thought we hadn't been seen and wasn't ready. But we're going in expecting a potential fight. I'll be ready."

"Okay. Fine. Cassie can be as stubborn as you. We'll go together. Just know you're welcome to leave when you choose."

An hour later, Maya and Ava were on their way home while Tori and Chance split up to go around the mall. From the back of the sports store, Chance had found two binoculars, radios with batteries, and a night vision monocular. He had hoped to find some ammunition for his handgun, but the store's scattered inventory was sports-related.

"Chance," Tori's voice crackled softly over the radio. "I'm at the northwest corner, right near the freeway. Except for one spot, I've confirmed all outside doors are blocked, either by earthquake damage or they're barricaded. There are at least two armed guys on the roof."

"Same on this end. A couple of armed guys on the roof, and, except for the south store where I got in earlier, all doors and entrances appear to be unusable. The shop at the end is damaged, but we might get in. It doesn't look like any additional barricades are set up there, so Chad's gang probably isn't aware of it. Where's the one spot you found?"

"It's a delivery space tucked in between the northeast corner anchor store, which juts out from the mall, and the northeast entrance. That entrance used to have lots of windows, but those are all busted, and inside I could see it was barricaded with a couple of armed guards. The delivery area has solid doors, but I saw a couple of guys go in and out. I'm guessing that's their main entrance, and it's probably guarded."

"Now we just need to know what's inside."

"And we really need to wait until it's dark. That's still a few hours away."

"Yeah," admitted Chance. "Let's meet back at the sports store in about 15 minutes. We can get something to eat and decide what to do next."

———

A quarter-hour later, Chance saw Tori walking towards the store from the north end of the parking lot as he approached from the south. He turned off his radio to conserve the batteries, and his fingers twisted the wrong knob.

Static. Static.

"Chad, do you copy?"

"Go for Chad."

"We're taking the girls back to the camera store now. We had a bit of an incident where one of them tried to break free again."

"Cassie?"

"Yeah. We had to rough her up a bit to get her to settle down. You sure we can't just take care of her and her friends now? Her coward brother's not likely to come back. And we could use some fun."

"He'll be back. Big T's supposed to be here late tonight. His guys will be helpful in keeping things in order. I suspect Chance will be back soon."

Chapter Fifteen

Infiltration

"**T**HE CAMERA STORE?" TORI asked.

"That's what the guy said. It's probably one of the smaller stores."

"Maybe we should listen more. See if we can get more clues."

"Might be risky. I'm wondering whether someone heard us talking earlier. I didn't really think about the fact that the radios are open for anyone to listen to."

"Wait! I wonder if he's talking about the photography studio on the upper level, across from the arcade games and bowling alley. It's a small place next to an Asian gifts store. We went there for some glamour shots a year ago."

"I'm familiar with the arcade and bowling area, but I don't know the rest of the mall very well. A small store on the upper level, with no exterior exit, would be a good place for hostages. He expected me to come for Cassie and used her as bait to lure me in."

"Do you think he really wants to kill you?"

"Well, his buddies didn't seem to hold much back earlier." Chance rubbed his upper arm. "And he added something as well. Normally they'd probably just push me around, but, with the stress of the last couple days and lack of any law enforcement, who knows."

"What'd you do to him?"

Chance's jaw clenched. "The vice principal asked me about some reported cheating and alcohol-related incidents. I guess it was my report that got Chad and his buddies suspended for three games. Football is everything to him, and with it being our senior year, he's been scouted and was expecting more scouts for college football. Our team was doing well enough to get into the state playoffs again, but when a couple of games got lost, that option was iffy. Chad blames me for the losses because I wasn't there to play, and blames me for him missing the scouting opportunities."

"Sounds kinda extreme."

"Yeah, but like I said, football's everything to him. Ever since elementary school, his dream's been to play college football and then go pro. He's really an amazing quarterback."

"So you blew his dream."

"Something like that. I'm sure his dad isn't happy with me either."

"What's his dad got to do with it?"

"His dad's a CEO and former college quarterback. An injury sidelined him and kept him from going pro. I think he's kind of hoping to live his dream through Chad. So, if Chad told him I'd gotten in the way, yeah, it's not a good thing. Word was that Chad and his buddies should've been kicked off the team, but his dad pulled some financial strings and got it reduced to a three-game suspension."

They sat in silence for a few minutes in the sports store, eating some snacks and drinking from water bottles they had found in the employee breakroom of a nearby clothing store. Searches of restaurants yielded empty shelves and spoiling food. Through the broken front windows, the sun touched the top of the mall a quarter-mile away.

Tori swallowed. "It's about time to go. If it gets too dark, we'll have to use the flashlights you found earlier to see inside the shop, and that might give us away. The twilight should be enough to keep us from being seen too easily."

———

A few minutes later, Chance crouched down along a familiar incline, lined with trees. He and Tori were close to the southeast corner of the mall. Various parts of his body tensed and ached from his earlier encounter. After a momentary search of the rooftop, Tori swept through the fading light to the shop doors. She held her hand up for Chance to wait while she examined the doors.

A minute later she motioned for him. He scanned to roofline and then darted under the tree cover towards Tori.

The three vehicle rolling doors were bent and buckled. On the left, next to the main building, Tori put a finger to her lips and pointed at the man door. A sliver of black revealed she had unlocked and opened the solid metal door a few inches. Chance wondered how the door had survived so it could be opened. He guessed the combination of the exterior hinges and its metal frame inside a narrow section of concrete wall, set between the garage doors and the mall, might have made the door less susceptible to earthquake damage.

Tori leaned close to Chance and whispered, "The door might be noisy. I'm only going to open it enough for you to get in. Then you hold it while I come in."

Chance nodded. Tori tugged gently on the door. It opened a few more inches and then resisted. Chance shed his pack and put it through first. Then his right side slid through. Turning his head, he passed through, but the door snagged hold of his chest and refused full entry. He exhaled and squirmed inside while his chest pushed back against the door's refusal.

A grating sound wailed into the twilight. The door popped open a few more inches, and Chance stumbled through. "Quick!" he hissed, holding the door open.

Tori easily slid through. A focused beam of light swept across the cars in the parking lot, methodically moving closer to the building in the twilight. Chance tried to pull the door closed, but it seemed to be caught open. He tugged. The door retched another grating sound like metal claws raking a chalkboard. Then the door released and slammed inward. Chance's left foot arrested the closing before the door hit the jamb. Outside, the spot of light jumped across the parking lot to the wall of the building, and the door settled softly back into its place right before the light caught it.

Slices of the fading light cut through cracks in the crumpled rolling doors and illuminated the garage only enough to see that various equipment had been violently tossed to the floor. A vehicle lift bent over in the second bay. Even without the earthquake's destructive touch, the shop looked abandoned. A wide utility elevator door occupied part of the left wall, where slivers of light reflected off bent metal.

Chance glanced behind him where Tori locked the push bar of the shop door. She motioned toward the back wall.

Warily, he inched forward into the increasing abyss of the shop towards a black wall. After a minute of cautious steps, his eyes adjusted enough to distinguish a black door offset in the dark wall. He pulled the door back to reveal a void that stretched out and down to the left. On the right, a door hung from its hinges. Around the door, the buckled frame looked like it had spat the door out. Beyond the door, a room sat in darkness.

Tori ducked under Chance's arm and stepped into the void. She tugged on his arm to close the door. He stepped in as the door shut and Tori's headlamp flicked on. First bright, then low.

"Good thing you found these lights," Tori said, her voice hushed. "We might've been okay turning them on in the shop, but with all the holes in the doors and that light looking for the noise, I thought it was better to wait."

Chance's headlamp swept right, through the door and into a messy office. "If the room wasn't used, it certainly wasn't cleaned up before they left."

Tori's head cocked. "That was the supervisor's office. As far as I know, it wasn't used. But that was a few years ago."

His light shifted to the void on the left where the short hall dropped into a flight of stairs. "You didn't say the tunnel went under the mall. How far will it take us?"

"Where else do you think a service tunnel would go? Behind the shops?" Tori took the lead and started down the stairs. "There are some access corridors behind some stores, but nothing like this. This goes under from one end to the other, with some side passages. There are some storage rooms, but mostly it's for accessing the utilities. There're some stairs that go up near the food court. And I think another access by the arcade and bowling center."

The stairs descended and opened onto a wide corridor that went right and left. Streams of water trickled along the edges and pooled into occasional small puddles. The air was still and tainted with a mix of bleach-based cleaning supplies and musty dust.

Tori turned left, and they walked past a large service elevator door on the left side. "That goes up to the shop."

They continued through the labyrinth of tunnels as their shafts of light sifted through dust. Large pipes of varying sizes, each with its own color, snaked along the ceiling in broken segments. Wires and cables writhed out of some pipes. The broken ends of other pipes were empty. Grayish piles of fine sand-like material piled below the fractured cement walls. Cracks split across most of the ceiling. In a few places, bent rebar protruded from shattered concrete.

Chance tried not to think about the tons of cement and building materials that waited to fall from above and bury him. Nobody knew where he was, and his body probably wouldn't be found for years. A shudder shook his spine, and he focused on Tori as she picked her way through the tunnels.

After several minutes, the chosen tunnel opened into a large corridor. They passed the crumpled doors of another service elevator on the right wall and approached an intersection. To the right, a staircase rose into the dark. The corridor continued on the left.

Tori pointed up the stairs and whispered. "This goes up behind some of the food court restaurants, near where the mall management offices are. We're about in the middle of the mall. There are restrooms near the food court. Not that they work. From what you said of the radio conversation, I'd guess the girls were probably taken to the restroom and then back to the camera store."

"We'll need to be really careful and quiet then. While Chad's guys probably aren't expecting anyone to come in from this way, I'm sure they're aware of it. When you get near the top, let's turn the lights off and assess the situation."

Cautiously, they climbed the stairs, which leveled at a landing where a single door occupied the wall in front of them. Chance was momentarily confused when Tori continued past the landing to the right and went up another flight of stairs. Then he remembered they had started on a basement level and had two stair flights to climb. Ahead of him, Tori's light flicked off. He touched the button on his headlamp and shut it off as he reached the last couple of steps. Dim light faded through an open doorway, silhouetting Tori in a ghostly blur. Beyond the door frame and a partial wall, a faint white-gray light sifted from above.

Tori stepped from the doorway and moved mouse-like towards the fallen wall. Chance followed, his ears hearing only the soft scuffle of his feet. Past the wall, moonlight trickled in through the shattered skylights above. The remnants of the food court spread out before them and extended to the right. Light fixtures, ceiling pieces, and shards of skylights had rained across the scattered and overturned tables and chairs. A cool breeze shuffled in from the left, the air dodging through the formerly large windows. In the far distance, the rim of the Wasatch Mountain range cut a rough edge along the starry horizon.

As if in response, a violent aftershock rocked the building for several seconds. Muffled screams came from the right.

Tori exhaled a held breath as she leaned close to Chance and whispered. "Sounds like they're not too far from here. We'll take the other hall that exits near the north-corner store. That'll be about as close as we can get before we have to go into the main mall."

Chapter Sixteen

Rescue

THE SHORT ACCESS CORRIDOR opened into the center of the mall. The north corner store jutted out on the right from the main mall. Overhead, several broken skylights—less than half as many as in the food court—allowed scattered moonlight inside. The main mall intersection was on the left, where the south and west wings of the mall stretched out into the near blackness. Shafts of gray-white light split down from the ceiling along each wing. Above the intersection, holes gaped through the twisted cone-shaped tower that had once risen above the mall. Fragments of windows and pieces of the roof clung desperately to the damaged frame.

Tori motioned beyond the intersection. Chance squinted into the half-dark. Broken glass glinted around store windows. A few stores had their gates pulled down, but most were left open in the panicked, post-earthquake exodus. Like the windows and walls, the signage was damaged. Just to the right of the intersection, on the opposite side of the wide hall and over a pile of debris, a partial sign clung to the wall, "Camera."

Chance felt elated. Finally, he would find Cassie. He took a step forward and halted, remembering Chad and his gang lurked in the mall's dark.

A radio chirped somewhere in the mall. Indecipherable voices and punches of static followed. Two shadows moved outside of the camera store.

Chance whispered to Tori. "Let's move to the corner store on this side of the mall. You keep watch and give warning if anyone else approaches while I take care of those two."

At the corner store, a clothing outlet, Chance swiped a baseball cap from a fallen mannequin and put it on backwards. He grabbed a dark jacket and pulled it on. The extra-large jacket felt tight, and he realized he'd forgotten to take off his pack first. He kept it on and strode across the hall.

The guard on the left flicked on a light and shone it at Chance.

Chance had seen the movement and covered his face before the beam struck. He deepened his voice and spoke with a gruff edge as he continued towards the guards. "Hey! Turn that off. Big T sent me to check on the girls."

The light flashed away and then switched off. "Sorry 'bout that." The guard sounded like an embarrassed teenager, but Chance didn't recognize the voice. "The girls are locked inside. Is it time for us to have some fun with them?"

Only a few steps away, Chance hardly dared to speak in case he was recognized. The two guards moved towards him to intersect his approach path. His fists balled tight. "It's fun time, alright." His right fist landed a reverse punch into the right guard's chin. A half step left, and his other hand hammer-fisted the left guard.

The first guard's head jerked, and he tottered back. His feet slipped on some debris, and his backward trip ended with a loud *thunk* against the floor.

The second guard's hand came to his nose as his head tilted back. In the faint light, generous moisture glistened around his eyes. A roundhouse to the fully open abdominals dropped the guard to the floor before he could call out. An axe kick whacked the guard onto the ground, where he lay unmoving.

Chance whipped around when something slid across the ground behind him. He turned and saw a small object rolling on the floor, and Tori emerged from the shadows across the hall. He looked back at the store. It was narrower than many mall stores, but like the others, only shards of glass remained in the display window. Several portrait and landscape photos lay vandalized, from glass ripping through them. The security gate was closed and secured with a padlock. Beyond the gate, the store was black.

"One of the guards probably has the key," Tori whispered as she neared the store.

A quick search found the key in the first guard's pocket. Chance unlocked the gate, pushed it aside, and pocketed the key.

"Cassie!" Chance breathed.

A muted reply responded from the back of the store's abyss. "Chance? Is that you?" A shadow detached from a black rectangle at the back and coalesced into a hesitant young woman with shoulder-length dark hair. She started forward, paused, her head tilted.

"It's me. I finally got here." Chance walked through the remains of the store's entrance.

Cassie ran forward and wrapped her arms around her brother.

As they held each other in the embrace, Chance heard her sniffle. "Are you okay? Did they do anything to you?"

Cassie pulled away long enough to punch her brother on his upper right arm. "That's for not coming sooner." Chance winced at the impact. Then she pulled him back into a hug, and with a choked voice added, "And this is for coming."

"We need to get going." He broke the embrace and looked at Cassie. "Who's with you? We need to go before Chad and his gang come."

Cassie nodded toward the back of the store. "Jenna, Malik, Zoe. It's Chance."

Cassie's friends emerged from the dark into the storefront. Even in the dark, it was easy to see that their clothes were dirty.

"Looks like we're all here," Chance said. "Time to go."

He led them into the cluttered hall and called softly. "Tori?"

From the dimly lit hall, a familiar voice replied. "Leaving so soon? And just when the family is all back together."

Chance whipped around. Chad and a half dozen guys stepped from the shadows into the broken moonlight cast down from shattered skylights overhead. One guy gripped Tori's arms behind her back while a cloth was pulled back into her mouth.

"I've got to admit," Chad started. "You're more resourceful than I thought. I'm not sure how you got past my guys, but it certainly made things more interesting." He looked down at the two guards lying on the floor. "Zane and Trent aren't going to be happy with you."

"Let the girls go. I know it's me you want."

"True, I want you to know how it feels to have all your dreams taken from you. When we're done with you, the only dream you'll have is to find a wheelchair and someone to push you around in it. And seeing how things are right now, it may be a while before you can get that."

"Let them go." Chance's eyes sifted through the darkness, scanning for something, anything, that might help.

"You're just delaying the inevitable. As for the girls, no. I want them to see what happens to those who betray me. And I promised the guys as soon as you are taken care of, they could have some fun with the girls. They've really been waiting patiently to show them a good time."

"You're sick. The world as we know it will never be the same, and all you can think of is your twisted idea of revenge."

A radio cackled. "Big T's approaching the outer perimeter with a dozen of his guys."

Chad held a radio up to his mouth. "Tell Big T I've got the prize and the girls. Fun time is about to begin."

Chapter Seventeen

Showdown

SIX HEADLAMPS TURNED ON, all aimed at Chance. His hand shielded his eyes and he was thankful for all the night games he'd played with bright stadium lights.

"Ahh, Chance, is it too bright for you?" taunted Chad. "We could do this in the dark, but I thought you'd like to know these guys have more than one score to settle with you now."

The lights made it difficult, but Chance recognized the same six from the day before: Knox, Slade, Blaze, Jax, Axel, and Rocco. Except for Rocco, each had rearmed themselves with baseball bats. He smiled at seeing bruises forming on the faces of Knox and Slade. Jax leaned right, seeming to favor his left side. Rocco held Tori securely in place. None of the six were smiling or laughing at him like they had on their previous encounter. The two guards from earlier were moving on the floor.

"Oh, good," continued Chad. "Looks like Zane and Trent will be joining. Cassie, you and your friends just stay back there in the store if you don't want to get hurt."

"Chad," Cassie's voice sounded desperate. "Why are you doing this? What happened to you? You and Chance used to be best friends. Now you want to kill him?"

Chad's jaw shifted. "No. I don't want to kill him, just to see him suffer like he did to me. He abandoned any friendship we might've had, trashed our dreams, and betrayed our team and me. Any chance of redemption was lost with this disaster."

"Let her and her friends go," pleaded Chance. "Don't do this."

The jaw clenched and then Chad said. "They're collateral damage. I've done what I can to keep them safe." His head shook. "Now, what happens to them is because of what you did."

The six teammates looked like eager foxhounds, their prey cornered, and raring to get into the fray. They glanced at Chad, waiting for his command. Trent and Zane pushed themselves up and stood with the other six.

"Do it," Chad said.

Chance rushed the middle, straight for Jax's left side. The tackle caught Jax off guard, and Chance spun him crashing onto the floor. Jax's bat swept wild in the spin and whipped against Axel's right arm, knocking the bat from his grip.

Using the tackle for momentum, Chance pivoted left and plowed into Blaze, grabbing the bat in the process and snapping it free with his left hand. The bat arced around and slammed into Slade's chest as his bat raised to attack. Blaze rolled around Chance and stumbled to the floor while Slade doubled over, his hands grasping his trunk.

A hard thump whacked against Chance's back, and he was thankful he'd left the pack on. Chance parried a wild swing from Knox. His bat flew down Knox's and smashed into the right side of the head. Knox teetered for a moment and dropped to the floor.

Chance whipped around, his back towards the broken display windows of the Asian store, and held the bat out in defense as he surveyed his opponents.

Knox was down, and Slade was still out of breath. Chad was still behind everyone. Blaze and Jax were getting up. Axel, Trent, and Zane were closing in. Rocco continued to hold Tori, but his attention was on the fight.

Bats swung at him from Trent and Zane. He ducked under one and dodged the other. A blur rushed him from the side, and he felt his feet leave the ground momentarily as he and Axel crashed through the remains of the Asian store's display. Chance felt tugs at his backpack and jacket, and heard fabric ripping. He rolled away from Axel and quickly recovered his breath. Axel also rolled away and jumped up to his feet, eager to continue.

Light beams swept around the store as Chance sprung to his feet and inched back.

Axel took a step forward and stumbled, as if strength had left his body. His right hand touched his thigh and pulled it back. The beams revealed red on the hand and soaking into his sliced pant leg. His face tightened, and he rushed at Chance.

Anticipating the impact, Chance stepped into and slightly away from his tackler. His air rushed out as Axel's arms crushed around his middle. His arms grappled Axel's back, and he twisted right with the tackle. The twist shifted Axel's momentum, and Chance let go, flipping Axel into broken shelves.

When Axel didn't get back up, Chance turned his attention outside the store. Trent and Zane backed away to join Blaze and Jax, and Rocco still held Tori. Chance looked around the store. Several six-foot bamboo staves lay on the floor like giant pick-up sticks. Various Oriental-style weapons lay scattered nearby. Not being familiar with how to use most of the weapons, and not wanting them to be used against him if they were taken from him, he grabbed a staff. He smiled as he spun it around, its weight reminding him of his lacrosse stick, and moved to the store's entrance.

Dust floated through the mall's air, creating eerie shafts of light that danced erratically around Chance's five remaining opponents.

Six. He'd momentarily forgotten Chad, who still stood in the background, arms folded, watching.

The other five watched warily as Chance moved towards them with the bo staff casually spinning. He smiled, knowing none of them had ever bothered to watch him play and show off with his lacrosse stick.

Trent and Zane lanced forward with bats they retrieved from the floor. Chance punched the end of the staff into one sternum and swung the staff around into the head. With a quick flip of the staff, the second sternum and head were walloped. In seconds, Trent and Zane were out cold on the floor.

Chance thought he saw Tori give him a wink and a nod. Her foot raised, and she stomped her heel into the top of Rocco's foot. His weight shifted back with his yell. She glanced over her shoulder and launched a back kick into his groin. He immediately let go and doubled over. She turned and whipped a roundhouse across his face. His head jerked to the side, and he dropped to the floor.

Jax turned to see Rocco drop and jumped back to dodge a kick from Tori.

Blaze angled towards Chance. The staff snapped in, but Blaze batted it aside. The bat rounded its trajectory and dove in from the top. Chance raised the staff to block.

Crack! Snap! Chance stumbled forward a step, with each hand holding a severed half of the staff. Blaze cocked the bat, and Chance saw it looked partially broken. He blocked Blaze's attack with the left staff piece. Another loud crack. Pain reverberated through Chance's left forearm. Behind him, something crashed into the broken window remains.

Blaze stepped back, tossed the bat handle, and came at Chance with several jabs followed by reverse punches.

Nearby, Tori yelped in pain. Jax's bat recoiled from her leg and then slammed into her sternum. Doubled over, she could do little to stop him from shoving her hard into the wall, where she slumped to the ground.

Distracted by Tori's cry, Chance miscalculated and blocked a feinted jab and missed its follow-up punch. The light beams sparkled for a few seconds as he tottered back and shook his head.

Excited, Blaze quickly moved in. Chance's left stick piece parried while the right arced across Blaze's face. Blaze twisted right while Chance's left stick smacked into the right side floating ribs. With his opponent hunched over, Chance shove-kicked him back into the wall. Blaze's head clunked back, and he slumped to the floor.

From Chance's right, Jax's bat dove at him like a bird of prey. Chance dodged left and snapped the right stick half into Jax's jaw. Jax spiraled and collapsed to the floor.

"Come on, Chad," Chance said. "What're you waiting for? It's just you and me now."

"Not for long." Chad moved towards Chance, his fists ready to engage. "Big T and the others will be here soon. I don't want to take away all their fun."

Chad feinted a left jab. Chance read the feint, and his right stick arced in. Chad's left arm dropped to block while his right hand caught Chance's left arm in mid-swing. He snapped his right foot into Chance's stomach as his hand twisted the stick-half free.

Chance dropped back, heaving from the blow. He pivoted left to dodge a front kick. His arms crossed high to block a downward strike from the stick. He briefly caught Chad's forearm in the cross-block, and Chance twisted his left hand over and around Chad's wrist to disarm him. The stick half clattered to the floor, and Chad slammed his left fist into Chance's side. A follow-up roundhouse to the hand sent Chance's stick flying away.

They circled each other, exchanging feints, jabs, blocks, punches, while light beams from the headlamps on the floor angled up like spotlights.

Chance read the feinted left jab and prepared to counter the reverse punch. Chad pulled the reverse and swept back in with a left hook. Chance's feet crossed momentarily as his balance wavered and the flashes of light cleared from his vision. A right hook swung in, and he barely raised his left arm to catch the impact. He snapped his arm over Chad's, stepped to the side, and twisted while sweeping his right arm across Chad's torso. The twist threw Chad across the floor and crashing outside the Asian shop.

In the cross streams of light, Chad's face looked like an angry panther as he sprung to his feet. His eyes darted across the floor, and he snapped up a fallen bat. Holding it like a fat sword, he charged like a crazed bull.

Chance easily jumped back from a wild swing and dodged another. He ducked under another, spun around, and felt the air explode from his chest when Chad's elbow slammed back into him. He stumbled and fell backward over debris as he avoided another crazed swing. Looking up from the floor, he saw light beams cross his attacker's face as Chad's flying leap brought the bat down from a high arc. He twisted sideways, and the bat smashed into the floor. Another quick twist, and he kicked Chad's backside.

With his balance already compromised from the flying jump, Chad let go of the bat to stop himself from face-planting into the floor. On his knees, he pivoted on the floor to retrieve the bat.

Chance snatched the bat and thrust it into Chad's abdomen. Instantly, Chad doubled over and fell to his side, his arms cradling his front as he struggled to breathe.

Standing, Chance raised the bat high into the dark and brought it down.

"No!" shouted Cassie from the store.

The bat splintered in half as it smashed into the floor next to Chad.

"I'm not like you." Chance tossed the busted handle aside. "Yes, my dreams have changed since we were friends. But I never intended to take your dreams away. It's one reason I kept playing, to help you."

The creases in Chad's face softened as his breathing normalized. His head turned toward the camera store.

Chance followed Chad's gaze and saw Cassie helping Tori up. Her friends followed from the store, and they approached Chance. He looked back down at Chad; the tension drained from his body. "I'm sorry my telling the truth hurt you, but you knew what you were doing and you knew what could happen. I wasn't the one who turned you in, but when asked what I knew, I have to live with myself, so I needed to tell the truth. But seriously, look around! We may have past choices we regret, but it's like our world is in a time-out, a reset. Nobody predicted what happened. Our past choices are past. What matters is what we choose now."

"What a stirring speech," growled a voice from the dark. "You must be Chad's itch he can't scratch, his pain in the butt."

Chapter Eighteen

Escape Route

A LARGE POLYNESIAN MAN stepped into the strips of light that crisscrossed in front of the camera store. He wore a blue professional team jersey with a Gothic-style letter T. His long dark hair was pulled back, and scores of tattoos covered his body like a second skin. Several similarly styled T's were prominent on his arms, neck, and chest. A handgun was holstered at his side alongside a large knife. A dozen similarly attired men of different ethnicities emerged from the nearby darkness. Among the men were several assault rifles, shotguns, along with swords and machetes.

Next to him on the floor, Chance heard Chad gasp. Chance felt beat and just wanted to collapse, but he summoned as much bravado as he could. "You must be Big T."

Big T's wide grin reminded Chance of a crocodile. He and his minions stopped in front of the camera store. "Ah, good. My reputation precedes me."

"What reputation? I hear you're just another bully pushing kids around to get his way."

Tori, Cassie, and her friends shuffled behind Chance.

The grin vanished, and his right hand gleefully removed the large knife from its sheath. "Your mouth will be relieved of its tongue. Normally, I just rid the world of those who don't agree with me. But I can see that Chad was right in wanting to make you live without the ability to achieve any of your dreams, and to depend fully on others." The knife pointed towards Chance's chest. "Chad's guys have done a great job fortifying this old mall. You've got no place to run. Tell you what, I'm feeling generous today." Two of the men snickered. "I'll let your girlfriends live if you can take things like a man."

Chance cocked his head. He did not know what Big T meant, but he was certain that letting the girls live didn't mean letting them go.

Big T's smile returned at seeing Chance's confused look. "We'll start with your tongue, since that seems to be what causes the most trouble. Then we'll move to other parts. Don't worry, we're not going to kill you." The smile broadened. "But you may wish you were dead."

Chance stepped back.

"But," continued Big T, his smile like a vicious knife edge, "any noncooperation on your part will result in your friends getting cut or shot in various places, and then finally killed. How long they suffer will be up to you."

The floor shuddered with another tremor. Behind Chance, one of Cassie's friends screamed and choked it back. A few of Chad's guys were stirring or sitting on the floor. They looked surprised, relieved, and intimidated to see Big T and his men.

"You know, Chance," began Big T, "you're right. Our world is getting a reset. Because of this earthquake, we'll finally take control of the cities in this valley."

The shudder returned. This time it continued getting stronger, and the shaking caused chaos in the dark mall. Unseen items fell, broke, crashed, clattered, and clanged. Some sounds were nearby; others came from the depths of the mall. Everyone crouched as the shaking increased. Beneath them, the floor shook and bounced. Debris rained down from the ceiling. All around them, steel and concrete shrieked and groaned. Dust began filling the hall like an ethereal fog. Nearby, a column toppled like a felled tree, and sections of ceiling crashed down.

Big T jumped back in time to miss a crushing beam. Several of his men weren't so lucky. The dust cloud billowed in a rage and engulfed the air.

"Chance?" Chad's voice was raspy and almost indiscernible amidst the noise of the earthquake.

Chance crouched near Chad. "What?"

Chad grabbed Chance's backpack's shoulder strap and pulled him down. Chance almost resisted, thinking it was another attack, when Chad rasped. "Down the hall, behind the Asian store. We left the emergency exit accessible. Use it to escape." Heading off Chance's question, Chad added with a headshake. "I'm staying here with my guys."

The shaking diminished, and Chance's feet felt more stable. He spun around to the girls. "Time to go. Follow me."

With limited visibility in the dust-choked mall, Chance took out his flashlight and turned it on. The thick beam penetrated the air only a few paces, and he used it to follow the wall past the Asian store. He passed a vacant storefront and nearly went by a narrow service door that hung stiffly in its frame. A dusty sign on the door read, "Emergency Exit Only." He pointed the light beam to the other side of the mall while he whispered to Tori and Cassie. "Go into the hall. There should be an emergency exit in there. I'm going to shut off the light for a moment, hopefully so Big T doesn't know exactly where we're going."

Big T's anger roared from behind the fallen debris. "Kill them all!"

Chance switched his light off and saw Tori shove the door open. They disappeared into the hall, and he pushed the door closed again.

Ahead of him, Tori turned her light on, and it bobbed down the hall for a short distance before it stopped. He quickly caught up. In front of the girls, the ceiling had fallen into the hall. Tori had crossed the pile to a metal door that had an "Exit" sign over it. The bent metal of the door told Chance what Tori would say before she spoke.

"The door's jammed shut," Tori said, her voice panicked. "We can't go that way."

"Quick, back to the main mall," Chance said. "There's gotta be another way out."

Their lights were briefly off as they opened the service door again. Splinters of light sliced through the murky mall hall from the right. Slivers of starlight split down from shattered skylights on the right and left ceilings.

"Go left," whispered Chance. "Try to keep the lights off as long as we can."

Chance led the way along the wall. Despite the dust, more light filtered in from the ceiling ahead. The air seemed to clear as they moved past another couple of stores where a cool downdraft came from the opening overhead. A small mountain of debris rose to the skylights overhead. Chance looked up and realized the roof had torn open, as if a large can opener had ripped through it and dropped the remains into the mall.

"Tori, Cassie," Chance said, "that's our way out. Up through the roof. Chad's guys probably have everything else locked up, or the quake's blocked things."

"What?" asked Cassie, "How?"

"Up that," Chance pointed at the pile that had pieces reaching nearly to the ceiling.

"Are you serious?" Tori said.

An assault rifle fired several rounds in their direction.

"Go around back and climb up. I'll try to hold them off." Chance quickly shed the jacket and slipped off the backpack as he followed the girls to the back of the twisted metal mountain.

Tori started climbing. "It'll be tricky, but I think Chance is right. We can get out."

Chance pulled the handgun from the pack, stuffed the jacket inside, and shouldered the pack. He pulled the action back and checked to see the round inside. The action clacked shut, and he aimed towards the flashlight beams.

Bang! Bang!

"They've got a gun," came the warning cry from the dark. The beams of light shifted and slowed in their approach. Several bursts of semiautomatic fire flew through the darkness. Chance heard the impact of several rounds tear into the nearby rubble. A couples shots ricocheted off something and pinged into the dark. He peeked around and fired another couple of shots.

Someone screamed in the dark. "The bastard shot me in the leg!"

Part of Chance felt bad, but that part conflicted with the satisfaction he felt. Above him, Tori yelled down, "I'm out!"

He glanced up and saw Cassie's legs wiggling as Tori pulled her up. Cassie's friends were next. More rounds pummeled the rubble and debris around him. He could see grayish shadows behind the lights. He aimed and shot.

Bang! Bang! Bang! Click.

Flashlights from three shadows fumbled in the dark. The action of Chance's handgun was locked open with the ammo depleted. He stuffed the gun into the small of his back and began climbing. His muscles complained at the exertion. More rounds raged and pinged around him. Another dozen rounds chased him through the opening in the roof as Tori and Cassie helped pull him over the top.

On the east, the early morning twilight cast the Wasatch Mountains into a rough outline. Orange and pink singed the tops of gray-purple clouds.

Big T's fury roared up. "Get them!"

"Where to?" asked Tori. "There isn't a ladder off the roof on the outside, and we're likely to get hurt if we try to jump or even drop off."

"Over there," Chance pointed to the south edge a short distance away. "I remember seeing a shipping and delivery dock like the shop on the southeast. It's half as high as the main mall. We can drop to its roof, then to the ground. Once on the ground, head south. Keep the cars between you and the building as much as possible."

Tori sprinted the short distance to the top of the mall's exterior wall and looked over. She moved a little east and motioned to the others as they joined her. They looked over the edge to a roof twenty feet below them, where the center section of the roof was swallowed in.

Jenna backed away. "I don't know about that."

"Chance," Cassie turned to her brother, "that doesn't look very safe to land on."

"Hang from the edge and drop along the wall," Chance said. "It'll shorten the fall, and the part nearest the mall's wall still looks good."

"I'll go first." Tori swung herself over the edge and hung from the top. She looked down and dropped. "It's good."

Zoe lowered herself over the edge and dropped.

Chance looked at Cassie. "You're next. If you can, get everyone to the far end to drop. This side has a further drop with the loading dock."

A chunk of wall exploded between Chance and Jenna, followed immediately by a loud gunshot. Chance turned. A man on the opposite side of the mall was aiming something at Jenna. "Move!" Chance shoved Jenna out of the way. A gunshot tore through the air as she screamed and clutched her left upper arm.

Chance glanced back at the shooter. Between them and the shooter, something narrow poked up through the skylight remains and was tossed onto the roof. "Malik, Cassie, you've gotta help lower Jenna down. I'll distract the shooter to give you time."

"No!" Cassie insisted. "We all need to go."

"I'm not leaving you, just giving you some time." Chance turned again and felt a hard whack through his backpack followed by the bullet's report. "Go!"

Cassie hesitated only a moment before joining Malik to help Jenna over the edge. Chance darted towards the skylight, where he saw some hands reaching through the opening. An AR-15 assault rifle lay on the roof near the opening. He ran over, stomped on the hands, and stooped down to grab the rifle.

"Owww!" The voice dropped quickly.

He heard another gunshot from the shooter. His eyes shot back to the girls. Cassie and Malik were positioning themselves at the edge. He gripped the rifle, aimed at the shooter, and fired three quick rounds. The shooter ducked in response to the shots. He pointed the rifle down into the gaping hole, fired more shots, and pulled back. A score of rounds flew up in response. He sprinted back to the top of the wall. The girls were making their way to the far end of the roof below him. He whipped around and fired several more shots. The shooter, who had just gotten back up, dived back down as bullets raked the roof.

Chance heard another high-powered gunshot. The shooter, who had been shooting at him, still ducked low. He quickly surveyed the rooftop and saw no one else. After strafing the wall behind his shooter again, he backed to the wall's top, sat and swung his legs around. After a quick glance down, he scooted off the edge and dropped to the roof below. At the other end of the building, he saw Cassie glance back before she followed the others off. He realized the simple instructions he'd given weren't simple in execution. The center part of the roof was more badly damaged than he'd realized. To get across, he had to follow the west edge of the roof, where a slip to the right would land him on the loading docks and the left disappeared into the building.

The rapid pop-pop-pop of automatic gunfire chased after him when he reached the end. The cement below him wasn't as far as the first drop, and he could see the others running out into the parking lot. A couple of them seemed to struggle. He jumped and felt something sear the outside of his upper left leg. The landing jammed his right ankle as it absorbed most of the impact. He darted towards the parking lot, grimacing as his wobble turned to a hobble. More shots raced after him, breaking windows, and plinking into the abandoned cars. The roughly broken asphalt added to the difficulty in speeding away, and he heeded his own advice by trying to keep cars between him and the building.

He was halfway across the parking lot when the gunshots stopped. Ahead of him, the girls rounded the corner of a building at the edge of the parking lot. A few moments later, Chance followed and found them collapsed and breathing heavily. Crimson red colored Jenna's arm and Malik's right leg. His own pant leg was moist red. He glanced back and surveyed the parking lot for a minute.

"Chance!" Cassie's voice increased in pitch. "You're shot too?"

"One grazed me. Doesn't look like anyone's following." Chance set down the rifle, swung off his backpack, and quickly removed the first aid kit. A bullet had busted through the end of the kit, but left most of the first aid supplies intact. He removed the handgun from his back and tossed it into the bag. "We need to take care of some wounds and then get moving again."

Zoe stepped in. "My mom's a nurse and made sure I knew how to take care of wounds. Let me take care of Jenna and Malik."

Chance offered the kit to Zoe and took some gauze and a roller bandage for himself. After the wounds were dressed, he put his pack on, shouldered the rifle's strap, and looked at the others. "Let's get going. Big T's guys will probably come after us soon. Even if they don't, Jenna and Malik need better medical attention."

"There's a hospital less than two miles south of here," Tori said. "That's probably your best bet. I should probably be going as well."

"Tori, thank you for helping me rescue my sister."

Tori's face darkened in the morning twilight.

"Yes, thanks for helping Chance," Cassie added. "I wish we could've met in a less violent way."

Tori smiled. "You're lucky to have a brother like Chance. If I had a brother, I'd want him to be like yours." She hugged the girls and even gave Chance a hug when he attempted a handshake. "I know you'll do this, but I'll say it anyway: Take care of your sister."

"Thanks again, Tori. I hope we meet again sometime."

Tori's smile broadened. "Just not when someone needs rescuing."

Less than a minute later, Tori disappeared across the street.

"Let's get to that hospital," Chance said. "I'll help you to the best I can."

Chapter Nineteen

New Faultlines

T HIRTY MINUTES LATER, A family of four joined them on State Street from an intersecting road. A woman had her arm in a makeshift sling. The man's right leg was crudely wrapped with strips of cloth, and he favored his side as he lumbered along. The son, older than the daughter, had his head and right arm wrapped with crude bandages. Only the young girl appeared uninjured. At first, they paused upon seeing Chance and the three girls walking in the direction they intended to go. The little girl immediately warmed when Cassie smiled and said hello.

"You guys headed to the hospital as well?" Cassie asked.

"Yes," the girl responded. "And Daddy says there's an e-vacuum-ation place too."

The woman smiled at her daughter. "It's 'evacuation,' honey."

The man added. "It's probably only limited, but I heard the military has a safety zone around the hospital and has been flying some people out. It's probably just some critically injured that the hospital can't treat."

Several blocks away, sun rays bursting from over the mountains illuminated the top of a tall building. Several surrounding buildings and grassy fields grew brighter with the warming sunlight. Reality took over when two Blackhawk helicopters flew overhead. In the buildings' shadows, the ravages of the big earthquake and subsequent large aftershocks were clear. No lights lit the building. Windows shattered and broken. Walls zigzagged with ruptures. Dozens of tents and canopies were set up across the fields. Several generators hummed in the background. Hundreds of people wandered around. A secure perimeter surrounded the entire area with makeshift fencing and military guardsmen patrolling. Several military vehicles were parked nearby, and ATVs were patrolling in the distance. Scores of people lined up at the handful of checkpoints that entered the complex.

At first, it seemed like chaos, but as they neared the complex, they could see four distinct areas. After passing through the checkpoint, the people were sent off into different areas of the complex. Some were quickly dismissed. The injured were sent to different color-coded tents and sections. Cots and stretchers littered everywhere. Away from the tents, body-sized white bags covered a field.

"It's set up for triage," Chance said. "Dad has mentioned that sort of thing. Those with minor injuries basically get to wait. More serious injuries that can only wait for a short time get moved to another area. Immediate life-threatening injuries get priority. And then there are those who aren't expected to survive with the available resources."

They approached a line that moved through the military checkpoint. Several soldiers patrolled the line and perimeter. Two soldiers moved towards Chance, their rifles held ready. One stepped closer while the other stayed back and eyed Chance and the girls. "No unauthorized firearms beyond the checkpoint. If you want to get in, you'll need to surrender your guns."

"Here you go." Chance started to remove the AR-15's shoulder strap.

"Turn them in at the check-in. But know there's no guarantee you'll get them back."

Chance nodded, and they moved forward with the line. Several soldiers guarded the checkpoint while others asked questions, assessed injuries, and directed people where to go. Chance handed the AR-15 to a soldier and did the same with the handgun from his pack. Two soldiers then asked each person a serious of questions while quickly assessing them. Jenna and Malik were directed to tents with yellow signs, while Chance was told to go to a green-marked area. After passing through the checkpoint, Zoe offered to go with Malik and Jenna to their designated area while Cassie went with Chance.

Chance watched Cassie's three friends head off. As he turned towards the green area, he noticed a soldier with a radio antenna protruding from his pack. A short distance away, a man dressed in hunter camouflage talked on a radio. Chance heard only a snatch of the conversation. "Thanks, Jason."

He walked over to the man. "Excuse me, sir. I met a Jason a couple of days ago on the other side of the river who helped me. Would you mind asking Jason if he met a guy named Chance? I'd like to thank him."

"Sure, kid." The man pressed the talk button. "Hey, Jason, a kid, a teenager, just walked up and wanted to know if you met Chance a couple of days ago."

The radio crackled. "Yeah, he came through on a search for his sister. Is he there?"

"Yep, standing right here with a girl." The man released the radio's button and held the radio out for Chance. "You want to tell Jason something?"

Chance took the radio and pressed the button. "Jason, this is Chance. Just wanted to say thanks for your help the other day. I found a place to cross the river and got to my sister and her friends last night. A couple of us got hurt from some gang activity, but we made it here."

"Chance, hey, thanks for the update. I've been wondering how things went. I've got a question for you. You said your dad was in Salt Lake when the quake happened?"

"Yeah."

"And his name's Doug?"

"Yeah."

The radio crackled. "I was talking with a buddy last night who's still in Salt Lake. Things are really bad there. Apparently, gangs are taking control of everything, and it's become a battlefield. He's trapped with an ex-army guy named Doug Morgan."

Chance's face brightened. "That's gotta be Dad. Can the military go in and get him?"

The man's face darkened. "Not likely. Salt Lake and the nearest cities are ground zero, with extreme danger and unlikelihood of survivors. Resources are being directed to areas that are less damaged and have higher chances of successful rescue and recovery. Basically, we're stretched too thin. I'm just former military helping coordinate efforts between the military and civilians."

Chance pressed the radio button. "Jason, can you ask my dad something?"

"I can try. What is it?"

"Let him know Cassie and I are together now and we want to know where we should go. Our house and neighborhood are gone."

"Sure. Give me an hour, and I'll see what I can do."

"Thanks!" Chance handed the radio back. "We'll get checked out and come back in an hour."

———

Inside a green-marked tent, a nurse checked Chance's injuries. Antiseptic and fresh gauze were applied to the bullet graze, and then he was sent on his way. He and Cassie checked on her friends. The medical personnel informed them that Malik and Jenna had been treated and should recover, but their gunshot wounds were serious and they would need to be kept for observation. Zoe opted to stay with them.

Chance and Cassie headed towards the entrance where they'd checked in. In the past hour, the triage complex had become busier, and several helicopters had flown in and departed. When they arrived at the point where the two radio operators had been, the military signalman was gone, but the other radioman was waiting for him.

The radioman saw Chance. "Hey, Chance. I don't have much time, but I can relay your dad's message. He wants you to make your way to your aunt's house in northern Utah County. When he gets out of Salt Lake, he'll make his way there. Hold on." Unlike before, a headset was plugged into his radio so Chance couldn't hear the other side of the conversation.

The radio operator listened intently and simply responded. "Roger, out." His face looked grim as his eyes turned left and right. His voice was hushed as he leaned closer to Chance. "Just between you and me, I don't think we're going to get outside help anytime soon. Our valley's a mess, and Utah County isn't any better. Transportation in and out is practically impossible. The freeways—I-80, I-15, even I-84—are undrivable, and the mountain passes are blocked with rockslides and landslides. Parts of I-15 and I-80 are flooded. Planes can't take off or land at the airports, and the railways are too damaged for trains. Helicopters are the only reliable way in and out, but getting fuel is becoming an issue. There's talk about setting up staging points outside of the Wasatch Front area and then bringing supplies and aid in from there. If that happens, it'll still be difficult to get adequate help in. You need to be on your guard because it's going to be worse than the Wild West before much longer."

"Thanks for the heads-up."

"There's more that isn't being shared with the public because of what happened here. The government doesn't want fear and panic to break out across the nation, but the info is leaking out. There are some fear-mongering conspiracy theories, but the truth is there are reports of increasing seismic activity on the west coast. Washington. California. Oregon. Some think they may be foreshocks to megaquakes. There are even reports that volcanoes may be waking. And the mid-west is also experiencing an uptick in tremors. The Salt Lake quake seems to have woken things up. I'm no expert, but I think things are going to get a lot worse before getting better. Regarding your dad, he's apparently gotten several survivors with him. The military is running a rescue and recovery operation." His head shook. "If you go to Utah County, be aware that the morning after our Big One, the Provo fault section got hit by a monster quake. Everything's bad. Just that some places are worse. I've gotta go now."

The radioman pressed his headphones tight and listened as he walked away.

"I think we should wait to see if the military can get Dad out." Cassie's head cocked. "But what if they can't, and Dad's stuck in there? Should we just leave him?"

From the far side of the triage complex, two Blackhawk helicopters rose into the air and turned north to Salt Lake City.

The corners of Chance's mouth lifted. "Not a chance. If they can't get to him, we'll go find him."

———

End of Seismic Faultlines

———

Thank You!

Thank you for reading *Seismic Faultlines*. With many other options to choose from, I appreciate your time reading my book.

If you enjoyed my book, please share your recommendation with others. A quick review helps others discover this book, and it helps me as an author.

Everyone I know appreciates the recommendation of a trusted friend. Return that favor. Please let your friends know through social media, email, text, in person or even a phone call. And leaving a brief review on Amazon is appreciated by me (as the author) and everyone looking for a good book to read.

Hope your day is fantastic, and thank you again.

Christopher Cox

Also by Christopher Cox

Hunt for the Fallen Star

A thousand years ago, a legendary starship with mythological abilities to traverse space disappeared....

Still reeling from his father's tragic death, Casey is persuaded by his brother, James, to join him and their best friend, Heather, as technical support for an archaeological dig in Central America. But after they discover an ancient starship and Casey inadvertently transports them across the galaxy, they find themselves lost in space and unable to return to Earth.

With everything alien to them, they must navigate a perilous star-scape fraught with space pirates, alien planets, galactic imperial forces, and foes with elemental powers. Amidst the chaos and political cover-ups, they discover the truth about the fabled starship—that its abilities of space travel are unequaled by any technology or spacecraft—and become targets of a galactic emperor's ambition to conquer the known civilizations.

With the galactic empire's sights set on Casey and the found spaceship, he must forge alliances if he's to save James and Heather, and escape. It'll take all their skills to evade the galactic military and prevent the onset of intergalactic war.

Non-Fiction Books by Christopher Cox

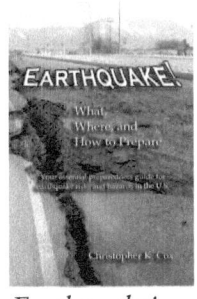

Earthquake! What, Where, and How to Prepare

Earthquake! What, Where, and How to Prepare was based on earthquake preparedness presentations Christopher gave. The book has three parts. The first covers the basics of earthquakes and their related hazards. Then, the risks and threats are reviewed for regions, states, and major cities in the United States. The last section goes into getting prepared.

Everyday Cybersecurity

Written for non-technical and "technology challenged" computer users, *Everyday Cybersecurity* simplifies computer and internet security. With the bad guys getting more cunning, it's vital that everyone who uses devices (computers, phones, etc.) to access the internet has a practical understanding and security awareness to protect personal information and identity.

About the author

Prior to working in IT for 16+ years, Christopher instructed at a helicopter flight school, installed security systems, and directed eight seasons of youth high adventure camps.

He enjoys being in nature—particularly the mountains—rock climbing, shooting sports, technology, and spending time with his family. He trains in Korean sword (Haidong Gumdo) and traditional taekwondo with his wife and kids.

Besides the United States, where he currently resides in Utah, he's lived in Chile and Australia. He's also visited Canada, Mexico, Argentina, Peru, China, and Mongolia.

Somewhere between work, family activities, church responsibilities, and home projects, he squeezes in creative and writing time. The novel, *Hunt for the Fallen Star*, was his first sci-fi fantasy adventure.

The non-fiction book, *Earthquake! What, Where, and How to Prepare*, is based on his earthquake preparedness presentations. Living near the Wasatch Fault zone with his wife, four kids, dog, and two rabbits, he has often wondered, what if scientists are wrong and the Big One is much worse?

www.ingramcontent.com/pod-product-compliance
Lightning Source LLC
Chambersburg PA
CBHW022022170626
46808CB00003B/1026